the
SPOOKSHOW

Book One

TIM McGREGOR

Perdido Pub
TORONTO

ISBN-13: 978-1505550603

ISBN-10: 1505550602

...still it is undecided whether or not there has ever been an instance of the spirit of any person appearing after death. All argument is against it; but all belief is for it.

– Samuel Johnson

CHAPTER 1

"SOMETHING BAD HAPPENED here."

"Like what?"

"Death," Billie said, stepping farther into the darkness of the derelict property. The air was damp and it reeked of rot and mildew and other foul things. Cutting through all of it was a thick sense of dread that hung in the air like a bad omen.

The other two women lingered in the doorway, reluctant to venture any further. One held a flashlight, the other a big camera. They exchanged glances.

"More than one?" asked Kaitlin. She trained the beam of the flashlight over the peeling walls.

Billie strode into the centre of the room, her shoes crunching over the grit on the floor. "A lot more. At least one of them was a murder."

Tammy adjusted the camera in her hand, jostling Kaitlin for elbow room. "How do you know that, Billie?"

"Because," Billie said. "The woman who died here just told me so."

A shudder passed through the two women in the doorway. Kaitlin, forever intrigued by anything spooky, said: "Where is she?"

"On your left. Touching your hair."

Kaitlin screamed and the flash on Tammy's camera popped, strobing the room in a white flare. The two women scrambled back into the hallway, alternately cursing and laughing.

Billie Culpepper was swallowed by the darkness when her friend scampered away with their only flashlight. The absence of light didn't bother her, not these days anyway. It came with the territory really, with this new vocation that she had accepted but had never even wanted in the first place. Seeing the dead. She wouldn't wish it on her worst enemy.

She didn't need light to see the dead anyway. Her eyes were now open to the lost souls that were there, in both the bright sun of midday and the blind pitch of night. Even if she squeezed her eyes shut, the dead were still there.

She did, however, need light to see where she was going. The last thing she wanted was to trip over the broken furniture and fall on something rusty and sharp. The abandoned house around them was a deathtrap. She shouldn't have come in the first place, even when Tammy and Kaitlin insisted on exploring it on their own. Pulling her cell from her back pocket, she hit the flashlight app but the beam was milky and weak.

Billie looked up quickly when the dead woman drifted too close. She wore a drab smock that was stained down the front and her skin was so white she was almost translucent. Dark fluid was dribbling out of her mouth and her thin hand clawed the air, reaching for her.

"Don't touch me," Billie said.

The pale woman stopped, her hand recoiling as if she had touched something hot.

Billie never liked looking into the eyes of the dead but sometimes it was necessary to get their full attention. This woman's eyes were cloudy and colourless, like that of a dead fish left too long in the sun. "What happened to you?"

The dead woman's mouth puckered but she said nothing. That in itself was unusual. When Billie opened herself up to the other side, the dead came running, eager to tell the sad tale of their demise. Their grievances, their unfair treatment, and their unresolved vengeances. The woman with the black blood dribbling off her chin remained silent. She scrutinized Billie with her milky eyes as if seeing something she did not understand. She lashed out again, fast this time, and plunged her hand through Billie's ribcage. Her touch was frigid and Billie felt the woman's icicle fingers lock around her heart. The pain took her breath away.

"Stop it," she snapped. Normally, the dead could be pushed away when they became aggressive but this one was strong. It took all Billie had to shove the dead woman away. The woman sneered at her with venomous eyes before withdrawing back into the darkness.

"All right, you guys," Billie called after catching her breath. "You can come back. She's gone."

Kaitlin and Tammy wedged themselves back into the span of the doorway. "Are you sure?" Tammy said.

"Yes." Billie brushed her hands off. She hadn't touched a single thing since entering the condemned building but her hands still felt grimy. "Seen enough? Can we go now?"

Kaitlin swept the throw of the flashlight across the room just to make sure. Something dripped from the bubbled plaster of the ceiling. "We're just getting started."

Billie sighed. "Make it fast then. I can't stay too long in here. It's making me ill."

"What do you mean? You're gonna be sick?" Tammy asked.

"It always makes me sick."

Tammy fitted a higher grade flash to her camera. "Okay. Just a few more rooms, then we'll go."

"Don't be a buzzkill," Kaitlin moaned. "Aren't you having fun?"

Billie frowned. "Chasing ghosts isn't a joke, Kaitlin. It comes with a cost."

"Jeez, Louise." Kaitlin passed the flashlight over the ceiling. They were standing in a large atrium with a wall of windows that looked out over the choked gardens. On the opposite side were two corridors and one closed door. "Which way?"

"Straight ahead," Tammy said.

Kaitlin agreed but neither of them took a step forward. She looked at Billie with a sheepish smile. "You first."

~

Sybil was her given name but to everyone, she was just Billie. The only person who had ever called her Sybil was her mother and Billie hadn't been addressed by that name since she was eight years old. On occasion, Tammy would call her by her given name but that was only to get under her skin. And that was before the accident. Tammy hadn't done it since.

Two months ago, her friends had confronted Billie about her odd behaviour, her sudden withdrawal from the world. Tammy, Kaitlin, and Jen (who had refused to come tonight) barged into Billie's apartment and demanded to know what was going on with her. Fragile and exhausted, Billie had blurted out the truth, that since waking up in the hospital, she could see the dead. And they could see her.

Conversation killer. The three women chalked it up to delusion and stress and, for the most part, they never spoke of it again. Billie didn't pursue it either, slowly coming back to the old routine and faking her way through being normal. Kaitlin was the only one who mentioned it again, intrigued by the paranormal, a lover of good ghost stories. Billie brushed it off as politely as possible. The world had turned upside down on her and the small circle of friends she had was often the only anchor she could cling to. Separating the two was an imperative now if she was to remain sane.

The dead were relentless in their need to be heard. They had tormented Billie until she learned to close herself off to them. It worked most of the time but the strong ones, the dispossessed souls that still burned with rage, these ghosts tracked her down like bloodhounds. There were days when Billie exiled herself to the little apartment on the third floor, unwilling to face the daylight.

Yesterday, Kaitlin had come to her breathless and urgent.

"They're tearing it down," she panted.

"Tearing what down?" Billie had asked. In retrospect, she should have just ignored the girl.

"The Murder House."

"What house?"

Kaitlin grew impatient. "The old ruins up the mountain."

There was no actual mountain. It was an escarpment that rose up on the southern flank of Hamilton, Ontario, adopted city to Billie and her small cadre of friends. Steeltown. The Hammer. An industrial giant that had rusted up and seized sometime in the late seventies before being beaten black and blue by recessions, shifting economic powers and corporate takeovers that slaughtered the pensions of its former workers. After choking on the fumes of its own death rattle, the Ambitious City had regrouped and signs of new life were popping up here and there like algae blooms on a dead lake.

"Up the mountain" meant up the escarpment, past the former rich part of town to the farmland above the city. The Murder House was halfway up the hill on a winding street choked by hemlock and oak trees. The crumbling manor was brittle with rot and overgrown with weeds. Its reputation as a haunted house was deeply entrenched, despite the fact that few citizens had ventured inside the place over the last seventy-odd years.

"Why are they tearing it down," Billie asked, idly curious but uncaring.

"Who knows," Tammy added, following Kaitlin inside. "But we want to see inside. Before it's gone forever."

Jen, Billie's oldest friend, was also there. She dismissed the idea outright. "What's there to see? It's just an old house."

"It's haunted," Kaitlin gushed. "I've always wanted to see inside. And this is our last chance. It's slated for demolition."

"And I can shoot it," Tammy added. "The inside of that place would make for great photographs."

At least Tammy's reasons were sensible. Professional even. She was a photographer and the thing she loved shooting the most was decay. She had a knack for capturing urban ruin that was beautiful. Tammy was probably right too, the interior of a place that had been abandoned for decades played to her strengths.

Kaitlin's motives were little more suspect. "We want you to come," she'd said. "So we can see you in action."

Jen refused to hear anymore, wanting nothing to do with the hair-brained scheme. Billie agreed. She was surrounded by the dead at every turn, why would she go looking for more inside a decrepit place with a bad reputation?

Disappointed, Kaitlin begged her to at least think about it. Billie had agreed but that was only to get Kaitlin off her back. When Kaitlin called earlier to ask if she was coming, Billie's answer remained the same. Kaitlin clucked her teeth and said that she and Tammy were going anyway. They'd tell her all about it when they came back.

Billie stewed over it for the next hour. Of the four friends she still had left, Kaitlin was the one she was least close to. An odd bird in some ways. Kaitlin had been spoiled and over-indulged by her well-off parents and, as a result, had difficulty taking no for an answer. Her interest in the paranormal had been a lifelong obsession, first stirred by an aunt who cast fortunes in the throw of the Tarot.

The clock ticked on and Billie stewed until the guilt nibbled her resolve. The 'murder house' had been the object of conjecture and local folklore since the Second World War. Murders were said to have taken place there yet no one had ever uncovered any factual evidence to back up this claim. Still, the crumbling house had stood unoccupied and unsold for seventy years. The odds were that the place really was haunted and her two friends were walking straight into trouble.

So off she went, to watch over their crazy antics in case

Tammy and Kaitlin ran into anything nasty. Riding her bike up the mountain proved tortuous and she disembarked halfway up, walking it the rest of the way until she found the street marked Laguna Road and caught up to her wayward friends. Kaitlin and Tammy had been relieved to see her.

The house stood back from the road at the end of a long driveway that was overgrown with foliage. A big Georgian home of brick with its array of broken windows and an arched portcullis that slanted to one side. All of it tucked away behind an imposing wrought iron fence.

Leaning her bike against the trunk of a tree, Billie understood why her friends seemed relieved to see her. Even at this distance, she could feel it; a clammy prickle of unease that crept down the small of her back.

Evil. The house reeked of it.

CHAPTER 2

IT WAS A dumb idea and Billie was not polite when she reiterated this fact to her friends.

Tammy agreed, ready to chuck the whole plan now that they were inside the house. Neither she nor Kaitlin were sensitives in any way but one didn't need any "gift" to feel the cold flush of dread that clung to the old house. The murder house, as it was known, simply felt wrong. Even rodents steered clear of it.

Kaitlin was having none of it. "You two are lame," she sneered. "This is our last chance to see this place. Let's go."

They gained entry through a service door on the east side. The main entrance and first-floor windows were all boarded up and inaccessible but the service door had been pried open long ago. Generations of teenagers and thrill-seekers had stomped in and out of the murder house over the decades. Inside, the walls were muddy with graffiti and the floors littered with bottles and trash. Like any other party location, there were discarded condoms strewn about in every room the trio passed through. Billie couldn't imagine doing it in such an awful place, even on a dare.

Tammy aimed and snapped her camera through the foyer and the parlour, working fast to catch the last of the twilight before night fell completely. They ventured into a large hall where their footfalls echoed up to the vaulted ceiling.

Tammy adjusted her camera again. "Have you seen enough, Kaitlin?"

"Nope." Kaitlin scanned the ceiling above, the tall fireplace at one end. "What do you see, Billie? Any ghosts here?"

No reply came. Kaitlin and Tammy both spun around. "Bee?"

Billie was doubled over, clutching her side as if she had just cramped up after a long run. "They're everywhere," she hushed.

They both rushed back, Tammy getting there first. "What's wrong?"

"It hurts sometimes." Billie straightened up and blew her bangs from her eyes. "Being this close to them."

"Ghosts?" Kaitlin whispered.

Billie nodded. She was uncomfortable revealing this much to her friends. They still thought of her as normal. Sort of. "Are we done here?"

"We should go." Tammy fired a harsh look at Kaitlin before turning back to Billie. "Are you okay?"

"Yeah. Just take a step back. I might hurl."

Kaitlin watched her friend with dished eyes, entranced by the hint of something beyond her ken. "Billie, what do you see?"

Billie's eyes were fixed on something in the darkness and she winced as if witnessing something terrible. "Faces sometimes, coming out of the darkness. Sometimes just shadows."

"Can you see them clearly?" Kaitlin asked. "Are they all gross and stuff?"

Billie took another breath, nausea ebbing away. "It's more than just sight. It's feeling. Emotions. It's hard to explain."

Kaitlin reached out and held Billie's arm. "Can you try? If it's too much, that's okay but, I've always wanted to know."

Shaking it off, Billie surveyed the large hall. Then her mouth twisted as if she had tasted something sour. "There's a man by the window, staring at us. The hatred in his eyes is freaky. He hates women. He's done bad things to women before. And he wants to hurt the three of us."

The two women snapped their necks around to check the row of tall windows that looked out over the gardens. There was no one there.

"Can he hurt us?" Tammy asked, a quiver of uncertainty rattling her skepticism.

"He might."

"Who is he?" Kaitlin whispered, as if afraid she'd scare the unseen phantom away. "What's his name?"

Billie shook her head. "He won't say. None of them will."

Tammy gulped. "How many are there?"

"More than I can count. I need to get out of this room."

Crossing out into the corridor, Tammy took Billie by the elbow, worried she might keel over. "Do they always try and hurt you?"

"Some don't mean to. But I can feel what killed them. It's like an echo."

Kaitlin drew up on Billie's flank. "So what about him? Can you tell what killed him?"

"Something to do with his lungs. Like T.B., maybe."

"What else?" Kaitlin urged.

"Misery. A lot of bad things happened here. A lot of death."

"So it is a murder house," Kaitlin concluded. "Who was murdered here?"

"I don't know. They won't come close," The nausea finally abated and Billie sighed as if to flush it out. "They're still afraid."

Tammy bit her lip. "I think it's time to go."

"We just got here," Kaitlin protested.

"It's making her sick, Kay." Tammy stopped in her tracks. "Haven't you seen enough?"

"Just a little longer. Please? Unless it's really bad. Billie, can we keep going or is it too much?"

Where the two young women had stopped, Billie carried on, shuffling toward a door under the staircase.

"Billie? You all right?"

The knob squealed as it turned and Billie swept the door open. Stairs led down into darkness. "There's something down here."

"Like what?"

"I don't know. Let me have the flashlight."

Kaitlin handed across the heavy Maglite but Tammy blocked her path. "No way are we going down into the basement."

"Don't be a chicken-shit," Kaitlin scolded.

Billie said nothing. She took the flashlight and let the beam ripple along the worn steps. And then she followed it down.

Kaitlin smirked and went next. Tammy cursed them both and hurried to catch up.

The cellar was clammy and it smelled of earth. Forgotten tables and chairs were pushed against the brick walls, a narrow pathway cutting through piles of trash and splintered wood.

Kaitlin followed close behind Billie, her knees jostling into the tangles of old furniture. "What's down here?"

"I don't know."

"Then let's go back up," Tammy hissed, bringing up the rear.

They kept moving. The pathway led to an arched doorway and they passed through into a large open chamber. A wide open floor of gritty concrete and damp limestone walls. The smell of wax mingled with the reek of dirt. Billie threw the beam of light over the walls and Kaitlin gasped.

Tammy's voice was barely a whisper. "This isn't good."

The graffiti continued down to the cellar but it was not the tags of vandals branding their names in fancy script or the defiling of property with dirty words by the addle-minded. These were symbols strange and foreign, crude renderings of animals and people. The paint dribbled down the bricks, giving every glyph the sense that it was melting.

There was more of it on the uneven floor. An enormous star inside a circle with candles fixed onto the five points. A pentagram.

"This isn't good," Tammy repeated. "This is freaky devil shit. Let's go."

"Hang on." Kaitlin reached down to touch one of the candles. The wax tip squished between her fingers. "It's still warm."

"What does that mean?" Tammy spat.

"Someone was just down here," Billie said.

"I'm leaving. You guys do what you want." Tammy turned to retreat but with only one flashlight between them, she faced a wall of darkness behind her.

Billie moved further into the clearing, past the painted line of the circle until she stood in the fulcrum of the five-tipped star. Lifting one foot, she kicked at the floor as if it was ice that she could break.

"What are you doing?" Tammy hissed. "Get out of the circle."

Billie stopped kicking. She swept the light over the tangle of debris behind Tammy. "I need a shovel. Or a hammer. Something."

"What is it?" Kaitlin said.

"Help me find something," Billie said.

They sifted through the trash until Kaitlin came up with a length of cast iron pipe. A heavy elbow joint fitted to one end gave the pipe the heft of a rude club.

"Hold the light for me." Billie took the metal rod from Kaitlin's hand and carried it back to the centre of the pentagram. Swinging it overhead, she bashed the thick end against the floor. The sharp reverberation stung her hands.

Tammy was close to tears. "What the hell are you doing?"

"Bring the light here," Billie said. Kaitlin trained the beam onto the floor. The concrete was cracked.

Billie shook her hands before gripping the pipe again. Another swing and the pipe cracked through the concrete and the floor opened up.

Even Tammy couldn't stay back. The three of them leaned over the hole that gaped in the floor and waved the dust away. Kaitlin shone the light down. A shallow pit opened up below the crust of concrete. Flaring up in the shaky beam of light came the twin hollows of a skull looking back at them.

CHAPTER 3

"JESUS CHRIST." TAMMY backed away from the pit like it was poison. "Let's get out of here."

"Wait," Billie said. "Give me the flashlight."

Kaitlin handed up the light and Billie angled the beam down. The pit in the broken concrete was a shallow hollow four feet deep and the human remains were propped up against one wall. Partially mummified, the flesh and clothing had dried into a brittle husk draped over the bones. The sightless cavities of the eye sockets were tilted up as if in greeting to whoever found it. Whoever the deceased had been, they had been down here a long time.

"Seen enough?" Tammy needled.

"Wait." Kaitlin leaned forward, pointing to something. "What is that? On the walls."

Kaitlin placed her hand over Billie's to aim the light at the walls of the sunken pit. Yellowed squares of paper lined the inside of the pit like some deranged attempt at decorating the concrete tomb. Kaitlin reached down to retrieve one.

"Don't touch it," Tammy spat.

"Would you relax?" Kaitlin said. "I want to see what it is."

Plucking one of the slips of paper from the wall, she held it up under the light. Fine print, like a page torn from a book.

"What is it?" Billie squinted at the print but could make no sense of it.

"A page from the Bible," Kaitlin said. "The whole thing is lined with it."

"Okay," Tammy spat. She snatched the flashlight from Billie's hand. "Now we're leaving."

Tammy didn't wait for a reply, immediately beating a retreat. Billie and Kaitlin scampered after her, each one gripping the shirt-tails of the one in front until they daisy-chained through the debris and back up to the main floor. Billie told them to slow down but Tammy didn't stop until they clambered back over the broken plywood of the entrance and into the cooling air of nightfall.

Halfway down the long driveway, they finally stopped and looked back at the big house.

"Remind me," Tammy panted, turning on Kaitlin, "to never listen to you again."

"Oh, like I had to twist your arm to go?" Kaitlin rejoined.

Billie stepped between them. "Stop, both of you."

"Did you at least get a picture of it?" Kaitlin asked.

Tammy lifted the camera slung on her shoulder, completely forgotten in the chaos. "Shit!"

Billie examined a rip in her jeans, torn against something sharp in their haste to get out of the house. The sound of crickets chirping all around them brought a sense of security.

Kaitlin brushed the dust from her hands. "Now what?"

"We call the police," Tammy stated, as if there was any other answer.

"And tell them what? That we broke into the place and, whoops, found a dead body? No way."

Billie looked at both of them. "We can't just leave it."

"Think about it," Kaitlin said, pacing the ground. "How much trouble are we gonna be in? What if they think we had something to do with it?"

"They're not gonna think that."

"Look," Kaitlin seethed, "We just leave. And forget we ever came here. Agreed?"

Billie shook her head. "We can't do that."

"This is your fault." Kaitlin pointed an accusatory finger at Billie. "Why did you bust the floor up like that? How did you know?"

Billie bit her tongue. There was no way to explain the magnetic pull she had felt coming up from under her feet. They wouldn't understand. She didn't understand it.

"If you hadn't bashed open the floor, none of us would have ever known." Kaitlin kicked at a pebble in the dirt. "Therefore, we leave it and go home. End of story."

"God," Tammy said, her eyes dulled to a faraway stare. "How do you think he got down there? Do you think he was buried alive."

"Who cares?" Kaitlin railed.

Tammy wouldn't let it go, reliving the whole experience. "Or all that devil-worship stuff? What was that about?"

Kaitlin waved her hand. "My point exactly. See? All the more reason to get the hell out of here."

"All the more reason to call the police," Billie said.

Kaitlin turned on her friend. "And what are you going to tell them when they ask how you found it? That a ghost led you to it? Yeah, they won't get suspicious at all."

"Kaitlin, somebody died in there."

"Twenty years ago!" Kaitlin said. "Fifty years! Does it matter? They'll find it when they come to demolish the place. It's not our problem."

Tammy rolled her eyes and Kaitlin fumed in a stalemate and then the sound of the crickets returned. They both looked to Billie for the deciding vote.

Billie pulled her cell phone from her pocket.

"Oh, terrific." Kaitlin threw up her hands. "That's just great."

Ignoring the outrage, Billie dialed but then stopped. "Do I call nine-one-one?"

"Of course," Tammy huffed. "There's a dead guy."

"Yeah but it's not exactly an emergency, is it? I mean, it was fifty years ago but now?"

"I dunno. Who else do you call?"

"Jesus!" Kaitlin was in agony. "We don't even know who to call. Let's just book!"

"What about that cop you know?" suggested Tammy. "The one who knocked you into the harbour. Call him."

Billie had already thought of that. She knew one police officer. More than that, he was a homicide detective with the Hamilton Police Service. He was exactly the person to call and, conveniently, she had his name and number in her phone.

The only problem was that he was the last person she wanted to call.

Ever.

She looked at her two friends. Kaitlin wore a mask of disgust while Tammy sighed impatiently, wondering what the delay was. "Call," she demanded.

Billie scrolled through the list of names and stopped at one. Ray Mockler, Detective. She thumbed the call button and listened to it ring with a single thought clanging around inside her head.

This was a bad idea.

CHAPTER 4

RED LIGHTS STROBED against the facade of the old manor, painting the Murder House with an even more sinister air. Two police cruisers idled in the gravel driveway while three uniformed officers stood on the wide steps of the main entrance. A utility truck trundled through the weeds to the side entrance, emblazoned with the words Hamilton Police Forensics Unit.

The three women cooled their heels near the patrol cars where they waited to be questioned, a thorny knot building in each of their bellies. When an unmarked vehicle crunched its way up the gravel drive, the knot in Billie's gut twisted sharply. She watched the car pull parallel to the forensic truck. Two plainclothes men climbed out and spoke briefly to the uniformed officer before entering the house. Billie recognized one of them and her belly flipped. They were inside a long time and twice Billie thought she was going to throw up.

She didn't want to see Detective Mockler. She couldn't wait

to see him again. It was confusing and it stung and it made her angry at him before he had even said hello. Their paths seemed to cross continually ever since the night he almost drowned her.

When the detectives finally reemerged from inside the house, they crossed slowly to the central drive but kept their distance from the women detained for questioning. Detective Mockler was young for the homicide unit, a fact Billie knew from Mockler himself. A topic of ribbing used against him from the veterans in the murder bullpen. He was handsome to her but perhaps not to everyone. The butterflies rumbled up in her guts again but when she looked up at him with a teeny-tiny smile, there was no return smile or even a nod of recognition.

"Tammy Lanza?" Mockler said, waving his hand for the woman to step forward. "Can you come with me, please? Kaitlin? You're going with Detective Odinbeck."

The two women rose up, bashful and reluctant as two schoolchildren told to step to the front of the class. Tammy gave Billie a scared shrug that seemed to plead for luck.

Billie watched her friends walk away with the detectives, anger prickling up her spine. Why were they going first? Was Mockler really going to let her stew out here even longer? Anger tilted sideways into fear, with Billie wishing they had all gotten their stories straight before the police arrived like they were some gangsters out of a bad movie.

They hadn't done anything wrong, she reminded herself. A little trespassing maybe. But they had done the right thing, calling the police in, hadn't they? Then why were they being questioned separately?

Twenty minutes later, both Tammy and Kaitlin were escorted outside by the detective named Odinbeck. The two women were hustled into the back of a waiting patrol car and driven away from the scene. They didn't even say goodbye.

Mockler spoke to the other officer for a moment before sauntering over. "Hi Billie," he said, casual as a run-in on the street.

Billie felt her mouth sneer involuntarily. "We didn't do anything wrong, you know."

"I know."

"Then why are we being questioned separately?"

Mockler shrugged. "Procedure. That's all. We live and we die by it."

Billie looked off to the road, where the tail lights of the leaving patrol car were diminishing in the night. "Where are they being taken to?"

"Down to Central. Their statements will be typed up and then they have to sign them. You'll have to do it too, I'm afraid."

"Paperwork?"

"Yup." Mockler rocked back on his heels, taking in the facade of the crumbling house. "Quite the mess you found, huh?"

"Dumb luck," she said.

"What were you guys doing in there anyway?"

"Didn't they tell you?"

"Of course," he said. "But I have to ask you too. Procedure, see? I have to cross my tees and all that stuff."

"They wanted to see the place. Kaitlin heard that it's going to be torn down soon. Is that true?"

"Far as I know."

"Why?" Billie looked back at the leering windows of the house behind her as if the house itself could offer some answer.

"Someone must have bought the place." He scratched his chin. He needed a shave. "What did Tammy and Kaitlin think they'd find in there?"

Mockler's tone wasn't hostile but it wasn't friendly either. It was bored and business-like. It irked her. As did the question itself. "The place has a reputation. You know that. They just wanted to see it before it was gone forever."

"Right," he said. "To see if it was haunted?"

Billie said nothing.

"So?" he said. "What's the verdict? Is it haunted?"

"Extremely."

"Anything I can use? Did any ghosts tell you who killed them? We got shelves of cold cases back at precinct that need closing."

The look in her eye was as sharp as cut glass. "Why are you being a dick?"

"I'm not sure," he said flatly. Mockler sighed then lowered himself down to the step next to her. "Procedure? Rules?"

"Sounds like you're making excuses."

"Maybe."

"So it's personal?" she said.

He looked at her. "Why would it be personal?"

There was a notebook in his hand, the spiral ring type common with students. He opened it to the last scribble of notes and frowned then he closed the book again and laid it flat on the stone slab between them. "How did you know the remains were down there?"

"Lucky guess."

"Billie..."

She looked at him again. Mockler was aware of her abilities. He just didn't believe in them. "You're not going to like the answer," she said.

"I need to put something down in the report."

"Let's say it was a smell coming up from the floor. That's actually pretty close." Billie expected him to jot it down in the notebook but he didn't stir. He looked out over the unkept grounds and tall trees as if he'd come for the view.

"Do you know who he is?" she asked. "The man in the pit?"

"No idea. I doubt we ever will. The body's been down there a long time." His eyebrow shot up at her. "How do you know it's a him?"

"Just a guess."

"Do you know who he is? You know, like, how you see things?"

It was her turn to look archly skeptical. "You're gonna believe what I say?"

"Anything would help at this point."

She wished there was something. A baffling urge to help him came over her. "Sorry."

He fell silent and the crickets chirped their mindless songs and Billie became all too aware of the space between herself and the detective next to her. Less than two feet. Think of something else, she scolded inside her head. "What about all that other stuff down there? The candles and pentagram?"

"The Halloween party?" He shrugged. "God knows. Probably just kids screwing around. Seems to be a trend, though."

She sat up. "What do you mean?"

"I've been seeing a lot of it lately. Devil-worship is a hip thing now. Especially at places like this." Here he cocked a thumb at the house behind them. "Places with reputations."

Billie turned to take in the expanse of the facade at their backs. It loomed up over them like a threat. "You know what they call this place, right?"

"Murder House? Yeah."

"Is it true?" she said. "Was there a murder here?"

"Not in my time. Any place that stands empty long enough becomes a haunted house. There's dozens of them all over town."

"Maybe the whole city is haunted."

"No doubt." He brushed dust from his knee. Then he tugged

at his tie, loosening it. "So. Aside from trespassing and finding corpses, how have you been?"

"I'm okay," she lied. "I'm good."

"Yeah?" He took another look at her. "You look a little thin actually. You taking care of yourself?"

"Thin? What does that mean?"

"Easy. I'm just asking if you're eating your veggies, that's all."

"Oh." She had a habit of doing that around him. Misconstruing a remark, bristling over something that wasn't there. "Well, you look tired, detective."

"Thanks." He smiled at the jab. He gathered up his notebook and got to his feet. A pop sounded from his knee. "You ready to go downtown and fill out a long boring report?"

"Not really."

"Come on. I'll get one of the officers to drive you down."

"Aren't you taking me?"

"I gotta stay here. Look for clues and stuff, ya know?"

She rose from the step and brushed herself off. "Mockler, how much trouble are we in?"

He squinted up at the house like he was trying to square its property value. "Not sure. A few minor things. I'll see what I can do."

"Thanks."

He walked back toward the side door. Another vehicle had pulled up and more officers were spilling out. He waved at her.

"Go make your statement. I'll catch up with you later."

Billie waved back at him but he didn't see it, swarmed by the newly arrived officers on the scene.

CHAPTER 5

IT WAS ALMOST midnight before Kaitlin had her phone returned and was allowed to walk out of the doors of Division One building. She thumbed her phone on. Thirteen emails and nine texts.

She was miffed. Kaitlin understood being questioned and having to give a statement. They had, after all, broken into the place but to have her phone taken away during that whole process had completely unnerved her. Her hands didn't know what to do without something to fiddle with and she found herself morose without the constant stream of distraction feeding her eyeballs.

The officer who took her statement wouldn't say anything about charges being laid, which drove her her nuts. She wanted to find out what they said to Tammy but she was still inside the station. Who knows how long she was going to be held up? What she wanted most, she realized, was a shower. The dust and the grime from crawling around inside the old house was making her skin crawl.

Kyle, her boyfriend, was sprawled in front of the TV when she got home. "Hey," he said. "Where have you been? How come you didn't return any of my texts?"

"It's a long story." Too long to go into now. She needed a shower and she needed to crash.

"I sent, like, twenty texts," he pouted. "I was starting to get worried."

Kaitlin surveyed the mess of empty nacho bags and beer bottles on the coffee table. On the TV screen, a demented killer in a Halloween mask slashed at the scantily clad bodies of nubile teens. Fake blood and bad prosthetic make-up. "Yeah. I can see you were real concerned."

"What happened?" Her snark had either gone over his head or was trumped by her filthy state. Probably the former.

"I'm going to take a shower," she said, drifting for the bathroom.

After scrubbing off the grime, she stood under the jets and let the water scald her raw. The tension of the last few hours melted off but the ball of ice in her belly refused to recede. More so, the awful image of those dry bones would not wash out of her mind. It flared up hot and bright every time she closed her eyes. How much worse would it be when her head finally hit the pillow?

The hot water faded and she stepped out of the shower. The

bathroom was steamed opaque but a clammy sensation itched her flesh and she wrapped herself quickly in the towel. The creeping feeling of being watched was sharp and she checked the window for peeping toms, knowing full well no one could see into her third story bathroom window.

You're overtired, she told herself. And freaking yourself out. Still, she toweled off quickly and shrugged into the robe hanging off the back of the door. Something moved in the foggy mirror. She startled and spun around but there was nothing behind her. She wiped a flat palm against the mirror to clear it and there was nothing there. Then there was a face. The eyeless skull face of the body in the pit.

She shook it off. Another symptom of exhaustion and a crazy night.

That's when the banging started. Out in the kitchen, the clang of pots and the boom of cupboards slamming shut.

"Kyle!" she hollered. What the hell was he doing, cooking up a meal at this hour? The banging and clanging went on and she stepped out of the bathroom and barked again.

The racket stopped. Silence returned.

"Kyle?"

No answer came. She padded down the hallway to the kitchen, passing the bedroom door. She glanced, out of habit, into the bedroom.

Kyle was tucked under the sheets, snoring logs.

Kaitlin froze. Someone was inside the apartment. She held

her breath and mentally willed Kyle to wake up but he didn't listen to her in his waking hours, so why would he heed her mental pleas for help now?

No more sounds issued from the kitchen. Maybe she had imagined it? Or maybe a raccoon had gotten in? The city was infested with them. She tiptoed the last three paces and peeked around the corner. Isn't this what those stupid girls in horror movies always do? Ignore the logical thing and venture barefoot into danger?

The kitchen was empty and still. No intruder wielding a machete, no animal rooting through the garbage. Her muscles relaxed and she mulled over the racket she had heard. Her nerves must be shot, she concluded. Her imagination stoked to fever pitch by the earlier events.

One detail stood out, one thing out of place in the otherwise normal kitchen. A dark object lay on the floor. She took it to be an article of clothing, a dark t-shirt Kyle had left on the floor but it was a bird. A crow or blackbird, dead on the tile. Its wings splayed out as if broken, the head lolling to one side and its glassy eye staring into nothing.

She recoiled in disgust and screamed for Kyle to come help. This must have been what she heard, the bird flapping around the kitchen, knocking things over. How had it gotten in? The window over the sink was open but the screen was undisturbed.

She hollered for Kyle again but he failed to appear and she decided then and there to break up with him. She couldn't think of a clearer sign than this. He was of no use when she needed him. She'd have to deal with this herself. Not that she knew what to do with a dead bird. What was the protocol for finding a kamikaze crow? Toss it down the garbage chute or call the city? Fling it into the neighbour's backyard and let them deal with it?

Gathering a big plastic bag from under the sink, she draped it over the dead bird and scooped it inside, careful not to touch the thing with her bare hands. What kind of diseases did birds carry? Especially crows? She twisted the end of the bag and dropped the whole thing into the trash bin under the sink. Kyle could deal with the rest in the morning. Then she'd dump his useless ass.

She had been careful not to touch any part of the bird but she scrubbed her hands at the sink anyway and dried them off and turned to leave the room. She had almost hit the light switch when the banging started up again. She spun around.

Every cupboard door stood open. Every drawer was drawn out to its maximum extension. Even the refrigerator door creaked open all on its own.

The trash bin under the sink rattled and tipped over. The plastic wrapped bundle rolled out and crinkled madly as the thing inside struggled to get out. The black bird flapped its wings and hopped across the floor and cawed angrily at her.

Every muscle seized up. Kaitlin couldn't scream or run or fight back. As helpless as those dumb girls in the slasher movies. The bird flapped around the room and the cupboards began banging open and closed and when she caught sight of the leering face in the window, her mind shut down and everything went black.

One tiny thought bubbled up before she blacked out completely. This was all Billie's fault.

CHAPTER 6

"YIKES," JEN STATED when she got a look at Billie. "You look like a zombie."

"Good morning to you too," Billie replied. Shambling through the shop door with a tray of coffee in her hand, she moved like the walking dead too.

The antique bell over the door was a quaint touch that Jen had installed herself, thinking it was cute. Peeling across Billie's nerves at this moment, it felt more like punishment. Jen, of course, looked freshly scrubbed and perfectly turned out, as was her wont. The Doll House was Jen's shop on James Street, her dream place to sell vintage clothes alongside her own dress designs. Up and running for a few short months, Jen was constantly stressing over her shop's finances but Billie had confidence in it. The place had an oddball appeal that reflected its owner's personality: bubbly and fun. Billie herself had helped with some of the renovations, as had Tammy and Kaitlin. Now it was their go-to hangout.

"Tell me you didn't go to that house," Jen said, hooking another dress on the rack.

Billie handed her friend a coffee. "We got busted."

Jen's mouth dropped open and Billie sighed. It was going to be a long story and she honestly did not have the energy to go into it. But of course, she had to.

Jen's jaw continued to drop as Billie recapped the events of the previous night. Interrupting here and there to clarify a point as Billie muddled the details, Jen was eager for nuance but Billie waved a white flag for her to let it go. She had been interrogated once already.

"See?" Jen said with a minor note of righteousness. "I knew it would be trouble."

Billie lifted the cup to her lips but all that was left was foam. "What was I supposed to do, let them go in there alone?"

Jen knew of Billie's gift. Or rather, she was aware of what Billie claimed she could do but Jen refused to even contemplate the idea, a position that Billie respected. Despite the fact that they had known each other since high school, the two of them simply didn't discuss it. An unstated accord of conversation.

"It's a wonder no one was hurt crawling around a place like that," Jen said, shaking her head. "Whatever possessed you to break up the floor?"

"Dunno," Billie replied.

"You must know. I mean, did you see something? Like a, you

know..."

Billie looked up in surprise. This was as close as Jen had ever come to discussing the ability Billie suffered from. "No. That's what was so weird about it. I didn't see anything. I just felt drawn to it. Like a magnet."

Maybe, Billie thought, Jen was coming around and they could actually discuss this bizarre turn her life had taken since that night in June. After initially driving her insane, this "gift" Billie had developed left her isolated from the world. The dead were everywhere and there was no escape from them and there were few she could talk to about it. Kaitlin was a believer but her interest in Billie's faculty was prurient. She saw it as a cool parlour trick, something to pull out at parties to wow the unwary. Tammy remained healthily skeptical. Even last night's shenanigans would do little to change that.

Jen was her oldest friend. If she could discuss it with her, or at least vent about what it was like to be eternally haunted, she wouldn't feel so cut off from the rest of the world. Keeping it to herself was poisonous.

"Have you seen this yet?" Jen said, lifting out one of the dresses from the rack. "It's new. The design looked good on paper but I'm not sure if it actually works. What do you think?"

With that, Billie knew, the matter was closed. Jen didn't want to discuss it anymore. Billie looked over the dress, a simple frock of blue with white piping and a nautical print. "The little anchors are cute."

Jen held the dress at arm's length to evaluate it. "I like them too. I was thinking about a whole sailor theme, ya know?"

"I like it," Billie said, trying to keep her disappointment from leaking into her tone. "You could add a jaunty little sailor's cap too."

"Could you see yourself wearing it?"

Billie scrutinized the frock. Too revealing. "I can't wear stuff like that."

"Sure you can. You just need to try wearing something that isn't black."

Billie rolled her eyes but she knew that her friend was right. Her wardrobe had become somewhat bleak in the last few months. She was hounded by the spirits of the dead, for Christ's sakes. Bright colours just seemed unbecoming. Still, she wondered if it was a tad unseemly to dress like a mopey indie kid.

Jen draped the dress against Billie's frame. "Try it on."

"No thanks."

"Oh come on," Jen pleaded. "It won't bite. Just try something different. Please."

"It's not me." She was trying to be polite. Jen would have to put a gun to her head to try that on.

Fortunately, the bell chiming over the door saved either of them from pulling a weapon. Tammy staggered through the door and flopped onto the church pew against the wall. "Hello ladies," Tammy huffed.

"Jeepers," Jen exclaimed. "You look worse than she does."

Tammy craned her neck, working a kink out. "I got, like, zero sleep last night."

Jen joined Tammy on the bench and patted her hand. "Billie told me about how the police questioned you last night."

"I wish that was the worst of it," Tammy said. "Are you drinking that?"

Jen handed over her coffee.

Billie perked up, concerned. "What do you mean?"

"The nightmares. All night. I just kept seeing that awful thing in the pit."

Billie nodded. "That was an awful thing to see."

"Every time I close my eyes, it's there." Tammy leaned back against the pew, her eyes slowly drawing to Billie. "Remind me never to doubt you about this shit again."

Jen rose and became very busy straightening the clothes on the rack, clearly uncomfortable at the notion. "I wonder where Kaitlin is."

"She's probably sleeping it off," Tammy offered.

Tuesday afternoons had become a ritual for them, stopping by the shop to catch up and make plans. The catch-up sessions often bled into the evening and, on more than one occasion, had led to an impromptu cocktail party before heading out for the evening. Kaitlin was often the instigator, urging Jen to lock the door so they could have the shop to themselves.

Billie looked at Tammy. "Have you spoken to her?"

"I texted her a couple times but got nothing back."

"That means she's dead asleep," Jen said. Kaitlin's preferred method of communication was often flurries of texts throughout the day. A lack of response was rare.

"Maybe we should check on her."

"Oh, I'm sure she's fine," Jen said. "Nothing ever bothers that girl."

Tammy was a coiled knot on the pew, arms folded tight and her leg bouncing fitfully. Her eyes locked onto Billie. "Did that cop friend of yours say anything?"

"About what?"

"About how much shit we're in." Tammy crossed her legs to settle her twitching knee. "The cop I talked to said we were in deep."

Jen ceased fussing with the rack. "Who are you talking about?"

"He was just trying to scare you," Billie said to Tammy. "I don't think we're in any trouble."

"How do you know?"

Jen interjected, repeating her question. "Who are you talking about?"

Tammy wagged her chin in Billie's direction. "That cop guy Billie's all moony over. The one who knocked her into the harbour."

"Moony? Please." Billie's eyes rolled.

"Mockler?" Jen turned sharply on her friend. "You didn't tell me he was there last night."

Billie shrugged. "Whoops."

Jen planted a fist onto her hip. "I thought you were going to steer clear of that guy."

"I am," Billie retorted.

"But you called him last night?"

"Weren't you paying attention?" Billie asked. "We found a body."

Tammy's brow furrowed. "What's the problem?"

Jen held her gaze on Billie. "He's engaged."

"So what?" Tammy said.

"You're being unfair," Billie said.

"Am I?" Jen's tone became flinty. "Is he still engaged?"

"I have no idea."

"And you just had to call him? You couldn't call nine-one-one?"

Tammy sat up. "Easy, Jen. We were kinda freaked out last night."

Billie took a step back, feeling stung. This was a sore spot for Jen but Billie didn't know why. It's not like anything had ever happened. She loved Jen to bits but didn't like her friend's air of moral superiority on the subject. It came off as judgemental and it made Billie bristle.

"Well you shouldn't have gone there in the first place," Jen said and went back to the front counter, ending the conversation.

Tammy yawned. "What's up with her?"

"Who knows. Maybe she and Adam had a fight."

"So much for our Tuesday." Tammy slumped forward, elbows on her knees and her head hung low.

"Why don't you go home and get some rest," Billie suggested.

"And see that face again? No thanks. I need an espresso or something."

Tammy got up and they waved goodbye to Jen and stepped out onto James Street. Leaves rattled along the sidewalk in the wind, blowing over their feet.

Billie noted her friend's lethargic gait and drawn face. "Were they really that bad? The nightmares?"

"I've never had ones like this," Tammy said. "I don't even remember my dreams but these ones? I can't stop seeing them."

They walked in silence for a moment and Billie mulled over the events of the night before. The Murder House was a bad place. Bad things had happened there and the place attracted more bad things to it. She had seen places like that before but she knew how to guard herself against its effect, the tragedy or negativity or whatever one called it. Tammy and Kaitlin hadn't. They had walked in unprepared and the place had left a mark on Tammy.

Tammy stopped walking. "Bee, did something weird happen to us last night?"

"Define weird," Billie shrugged.

"I don't know if I totally believe this stuff. Or what you can do. But did something bad happen to us in that place? Like spooky bad?"

"No. Not the way you mean. I would have seen it, you know?" Billie snaked her hand through Tammy's elbow and resumed their momentum. "But what we found? That was traumatic. Horrifying. It's gonna have an effect. That's normal."

"Okay. Good." Tension seemed to drain out of Tammy. "I just needed to know."

"You'll be okay." Billie gave her a squeeze, relieved to see her friend relax. Tammy would be all right. She was level-headed and skeptical about all of this stuff. Kaitlin was a different story however. Her interest in the paranormal bordered on the perverse.

"Let's check on Kaitlin," Billie said. Tammy agreed and they picked up the pace, marching into the wind.

CHAPTER 7

THE TECH CREW sent over two dozen digital photographs of the crime scene. Detective Mockler printed seven of them and pinned them to the cubicle wall. Three were wide angles of the basement, lit strongly to reveal the strange symbols painted onto the brick. Another was of the pentagram on the floor and the last three photographs were of the skeletal remains nestled into the pit.

Hammering the keyboard, he ran an image search for satanic symbols or hex signs, looking for anything that matched the cryptic runes found at the scene. None of the images matched and after a while, his eyes blurred at the scrolling tabs of pictures.

"Do you have to hang that ugly shit up?"

Mockler spun around to find Odinbeck leaning against the cubicle wall, sneering at his newly pinned photographs. "You don't like my decor?"

Odinbeck harrumphed. "How about some plain old pin-up girls? Anything but that gruesome shit."

"Gruesome but necessary," Mockler said, scrolling through another page of arcane symbols.

"What are you doing?"

"Wasting my time looking for anything that might match the stuff we found."

"Right. Good old Murder House." Odinbeck leaned forward to squint at one of the prints. "That one there looks familiar."

The senior detective pointed at one symbol that resembled four arrows hatched across a crescent moon. Mockler pulled it from the wall. "Where do you recognize it from?"

"Don't remember." Odinbeck scratched his head. "I don't think it was a case. Hell, all this voodoo shit, it coulda been from a Black Sabbath record."

"Think, Odin. Scratch that puddle in your skull."

The older detective shrugged. "Alice Cooper?"

"Who?"

"Jesus, kid. You're killing me," Odinbeck rolled his eyes. "Forget the graffiti. It's just kids doing stupid shit."

"It's more than that," Mockler countered. "You remember the dead body that Hoffman got the call on? These weird markings were there too."

Odinbeck shrugged. "It was an abandoned property and the D.B. was a squatter. Again, kids tagging crazy shit on the walls. It doesn't mean anything."

"But there were other incidents too. The dead body under the foot bridge three months ago. More pentagrams and runes. Same with the murder-suicide Edwards pulled on Kenilworth. Weirdo devil-worship stuff all over the walls."

"So what are you getting at?" Odinbeck scoffed. "We got some Satanic cult running around killing people?"

"I don't know." Mockler nodded at the photos on the wall. "But that's why I'm looking."

Odinbeck straightened up. "Drop that stuff. The coroner called. We can go see Skinny."

Skinny was the nickname Odinbeck had christened the unidentified remains found in the pit. Mockler pulled his jacket from the back of his chair. "Have they found anything?"

"Yeah, we totally lucked out. Turns out our D.B. is Jimmy Hoffa."

Mockler smiled like the joke was funny, trying to remember who Jimmy Hoffa was.

~

Traversing the corridor to the examination room, Detective Mockler checked his gut at the door. He hated this aspect of the job. Odinbeck huffed alongside him, bantering away and cracking lame jokes as they went. The senior detective's distaste for the coroner visit was masked under easy banter where Mockler's ran the opposite way, drifting into stony silence.

Pushing through a set of double doors, they entered an anteroom where a woman leaned against the front desk, cleaning her glasses. She looked up as the men entered. "Hello detectives," she said.

"Marla, how you been?" Odinbeck nodded as he approached.

"Busy, as always." The woman smiled, revealing a gap between her eye teeth. She looked at Mockler. "How are you, Ray?"

"Good." Mockler looked around the space. "Is Greg joining us?"

"He's away at a conference," Marla said. "I'll take you through."

Odinbeck huffed. "Where's Greg this time? Vegas?"

"Montreal." Marla tucked a clipboard under one arm and gestured for the detectives to follow. "This way."

They followed the Deputy Coroner into a brightly lit examining room. The tables and cabinets were stainless steel and the terrazzo floor was graded slightly to a drain in the centre of the room. A steel door at the back led to the cold room.

Mockler tried not to swallow whenever he was inside this place. The smell of it, a nauseating mix of death and disinfectant, made him dizzy. He girded himself for the viewing and tried not to look at the exit.

Marla rolled a table to the centre of the room and positioned it under the heavy bank of lights overhead. A thin plastic sheet was draped over a mound on the table. Taking hold of one corner of the sheet, she looked at the men. "Ready?"

"No," Mockler said. "But go ahead."

The sheet crinkled as it was peeled back to reveal the remains underneath. It was little more than a skeleton, the flesh dried to dark leather that draped from the bones. Strands of hair clung to the boiled-looking skull and some of the teeth were missing. At first glance, it looked fake to Mockler, like a Halloween prop.

"So." Odinbeck leaned forward but didn't move any closer to the thing on the table. "What's the skinny on Skinny?"

Marla consulted her clipboard. "Male. Caucasian. Approximate age, thirty to fifty."

"That's it?" Odinbeck said.

"So far. As you can see, there's not a lot left to go on."

Mockler ventured in a step. "Cause of death?"

"Not yet," Marla said. "There are no visible signs of trauma. And with most of the soft tissue gone or desiccated, it's going to take a while to even hazard a guess. I'm not even sure if the victim was dead when he was placed in that hole."

Mockler's eyes widened. "You think he was buried alive?"

"Some of the fingernails have been torn off. That may have been caused by trying to claw his way out."

"Gruesome," Odinbeck sneered. "You find anything on the body? Clothes or jewelry?"

"No jewelry. A few shreds of clothing." The deputy coroner retrieved a shallow plastic tub from a shelf and laid it on the table. Inside were frayed patches of stained cloth. Marla carefully lifted out a limp swath of checkered material. "This is what's left of the shirt. There's a label here."

Mockler leaned in close to read the faded print. "Sears?"

"Yup," Marla confirmed.

"Jeez, that narrows it down," the older detective griped. "So how long was Skinny in the hole?"

"I'm still working on that. A while, I'd say. Ten years, maybe longer."

"What about DNA?" Mockler asked.

"We could try but it would be a shot in the dark to find a match somewhere." Marla laid the tattered fabric back down. "Once it makes its way through the backlog at the lab, that is."

Mockler sighed. "How bad is it now?"

"Oh, they'd get around to this in about eighteen months."

Odinbeck shook his head and stepped away. "So we got nothing? Great. Another cold case to hang around our necks."

"There is one thing." Marla retreated to the desk and came back with another tray but this one was much smaller. "But I'm not promising anything."

Mockler took the tray and both detectives puzzled over its contents. A dark brown mass, like a patch of dried leather. "What is it?"

"It was a billfold," Marla said. "I think. I'm humidifying it to make it supple before picking it apart. There might, and I stress the word 'might', be some identification in there."

"Awesome," Mockler beamed. He felt his colleague sneer at

his terminology and wondered briefly about requesting a new partner.

"Don't get too excited," the coroner cautioned. "Even if I can separate it without it crumbling to pieces, the printed matter may not be legible."

"It's better than nothing," Mockler said. He was relieved at the potential break but eager to get out of this antiseptic room. The body on the table remained a John Doe and that meant that, for today at least, he would be spared the awful task of tracking down a family member and giving them the bad news. It was the toughest part of the job, the one task that made him question his ability to endure the duty any longer. There were plenty of other doubts, other frustrations that left him bitter and willing to quit but informing a family of a death was harrowing. His personal record of such tasks was twenty-seven. And he was the youngest member of the homicide unit. How the hell was he going to manage another ten or twenty years of this?

"Thanks, Marla," Odinbeck said. "Let us know how it goes with the billfold."

Mockler raised an eyebrow at how quickly Odinbeck made for the door. He seemed even more eager to skedaddle.

"One last thing," Marla said, tugging a page from her clipboard. "I believe you asked for this, Ray."

"What is it?" Mockler asked, taking the document from her.

"A test on the substance used to paint the walls with."

Odinbeck grimaced. "What, the pentagrams and shit?"

"Yeah." Mockler skimmed the information but it was dense and technical. "What is it?"

"Blood."

The older detective groaned. More bad news. Mockler ignored the man and looked at the medical examiner. "Do you know what kind of blood? I mean, human or animal or whatever?"

"An ungulate. Of the Suidae family."

"Right," Mockler nodded. "And in English, that's….?"

"Pig's blood."

"Gotcha. Thanks." Mockler smiled and made for the exit. Pushing through the doors, he clocked the sour look on Odinbeck's face. "What?"

"You just had to ask that, didn't you?" Odinbeck huffed for the nearest exit sign. "Pig's blood? Like this shit isn't bad enough?"

CHAPTER 8

"KAITLIN'S NOT HOME," Kyle said, propping open the apartment door.

"Where is she?" Billie asked, annoyed at how long Kaitlin's boyfriend had taken to answer her knock.

"I dunno." Kyle's face looked drawn like he hadn't slept. "She was gone when I got up."

Tammy rose up on her toes, trying to see past Kyle into the apartment. "She didn't leave a note or anything?"

"Nothing."

A cold draft blew out from the open apartment door. It washed over Billie. "Is she all right?"

"She's been acting kinda weird." Kyle looked at his watch. "Listen, I'm just heading out. I'll tell Kaitlin you stopped by."

"Something isn't right," Billie said.

Tammy clicked her teeth. She wasn't a fan of Kaitlin's boyfriend. None of them were. "Have you texted her?"

"Duh?" Kyle shrugged. "She's not answering."

Billie shivered. The clammy feeling of dread continued to seep out of the apartment. "This is all wrong."

"What do you mean?" Tammy asked.

"Excuse me." Billie pushed past Kyle and barged into the apartment.

"Hey!"

Tammy startled at her friend's rudeness, then scurried in after her.

"Hey," Kyle groaned. "I gotta go to work."

Billie marched into the kitchen and planted herself in the centre of the room. Whatever she had felt at the doorway was even stronger here. Tammy came up behind her, looking the room over. "Billie, what is it?"

Kyle lumbered after them and Billie turned on him. "Kyle, what's been going on here?"

"Nothing's going on."

Tammy took her friend's elbow. "What is it?"

"Something has been here." Billie looked at Kyle again. "What has Kaitlin been up to?"

"Damned if I know," he said. "She's barely spoken to me. She was up all night."

"Kyle, have you seen anything weird? Or sensed anything?"

"Like what?"

"I don't know. Anything out of the ordinary."

"No," he said, glancing at his watch again.

Billie wasn't surprised. Unless they were keenly sensitive, men were often blind to forces outside of the norm. Whatever it was that had set off alarm bells in her gut was white noise to Kaitlin's boyfriend. "Why was she up all night?"

"That's what I'd like to know," he said. "Look, I gotta run. If you guys want to wait for Kaitlin, that's fine with me."

Tammy dropped into a chair at the kitchen table. "Have you called her parents? Maybe she went there."

"Oh no," Billie said, marching out of the room.

"What now?" Kyle rolled his eyes and followed her.

The living room was a mess. Two blankets were hanging off the couch and the coffee table was cluttered with dirty dishes and cups as if someone had camped out here. Billie stood in the middle of the room, slowly scanning over the space. Moving aside an empty bag of chips, Billie plucked two books from the mess. Her mouth grimaced and then she tossed the books onto a chair.

"What is it?" Tammy retrieved one of the books and looked at the cover. *Secrets of the Paranormal.* The garish font of the title hovered over the image of a ghostly-looking woman.

Billie began rummaging through the table, knocking the mess to the floor. "Where is it?"

"What the hell?" Kyle spat.

Tammy moved closer. "What are you looking for?"

Billie froze, then dropped abruptly to her knees and reached under the couch.

"You guys need to leave," Kyle stated. "Like, now."

The woman on her knees grunted like a fisherman getting a bite on the line. She dragged something out from under the couch. A flat board with numbers and letters in a stylized script. Billie took a deep breath. "Kaitlin, you idiot."

Tammy hovered over her friend. "Is that a Ouija board?"

Billie turned on the boyfriend. "Kyle, what the hell has Kaitlin been doing?"

"I don't know!" He nodded at the board at Billie's knees. "I've never even seen that before."

Tammy knelt down to whisper. "It's just a stupid game, Billie. Goofy kid's stuff."

"Grab that bag for me." Billie ducked low, stretching her arm back under the couch. She strained for a moment before coming up with the planchette piece for the board.

Tammy retrieved a plastic shopping bag from the mess on the table and Billie dumped the board and the pointer into it. She ransacked the table and the couch for more books, picking out the titles pertaining to the paranormal or the occult. These she dropped into the bag and got to her feet. "Kyle, you need to call me the minute Kaitlin comes home."

He looked at the bag. "What are you doing with her stuff?"

"Getting rid of it." Billie motioned for Tammy to follow and marched for the door.

"You can't just take her things."

"Call me when she shows up." Billie didn't even look back.

Tammy gave Kyle a sympathetic shrug before scooting out the door.

~

"That was a bit much," Tammy said once they hit the street. She hurried to match Billie's pace. "Don't you think?"

"No."

"What are you going to do with that thing?"

"Get rid of it."

"Billie, slow down." Tammy tugged her friend's arm. "What's the big deal? It's just a dumb game."

"It's not." Billie took a breath. "It's dangerous, especially for someone like Kaitlin."

"Oh come on. How could it be dangerous?"

"Kaitlin's always been obsessed with this stuff. I think she might even have some kind of ability. I don't know."

Tammy stepped back. "Ability? Like you?"

"Not like me. But she has something. She's open to stuff. I don't know how to explain it."

"So what was she doing with the board? Talking to a ghost?"

"Trying to." Billie looked up at the sky. "I think something followed Kaitlin home last night."

Tammy stiffened. "Like what?"

"You know what," Billie said. "I could feel it back there. It was all over her apartment."

A shudder rattled through Tammy. "There's a ghost in there?"

"It's gone now. I think it's attached itself to Kaitlin."

"Oh God." Tammy rubbed her eyes. "Billie, this is a little crazy."

"I know. I'm sorry."

A wind kicked up out of nowhere, blowing dust up the street. Tammy squinted at the gust, then looked at her friend. "So what do we do?"

Billie stepped over to where a dumpster sat at the curb, waiting to be collected. She lifted the heavy lid and tossed the bag inside. "Try and find Kaitlin. Before she does something stupid."

Tammy's brow creased with worry. "Aren't you supposed to bury Ouija boards? Or leave them on a church step or something?"

"I have no idea." Billie brushed her hands and continued on. "Come on."

CHAPTER 9

KAITLIN HAD SIMPLY vanished.

Billie flopped on the ratty couch and propped her feet up on the table. She and Tammy had spent the rest of the day checking Kaitlin's work and visiting all the friends they could think of. No one had seen her. Ditto her parents. Returning home spent and frustrated to her small apartment over the abandoned department store, Billie opened the last beer left in the fridge and tried not to panic about her friend.

Sort-of-friend. To be honest, she and Kaitlin had never been close. She was more Tammy's friend, from her club days. Kaitlin was a Hamiltonian blue-blood slumming it with the working class for as long as it amused her. And yet, when Billie's bizarre ability had surfaced after a lifetime of repression, Kaitlin had been the only one to believe her. As it turned out, Kaitlin was a devourer of badly written books about Aleister Crowley and alien abductions and "true" ghost stories, along with an unhealthy diet of conspiracy theories and angel worship.

Billie had been grateful at first to have someone believe her at a time when her life imploded and she questioned her own sanity. Kaitlin was suddenly her new best friend, wanting to hang out all the time where before she had had little time for Billie's sullen temperament. Then the questions became urgent. *What was it like to see the dead? How did she communicate with them? Could Billie teach her how to do it too?* When Kaitlin mentioned that a friend of hers was working in film production, she urged Billie to go talk to them about getting her own psychic TV show. That was the tipping point. Billie had begun pulling back, feeling betrayed at her new "bestie's" ambition for fame by proxy.

Finding the Ouija board hadn't been all that shocking. What was shocking was the amount of residual energy rippling through Kaitlin and Kyle's apartment. The place was thrumming with it. Whatever spirit they had stirred up at the Murder House had followed Kaitlin home. Hell, Billie thought, Kaitlin would have welcomed it with open arms.

And now Kaitlin was gone and Billie's fears tipped over into the worst-case-scenario category. She had even gone back to Kaitlin's building in hopes of picking up the spirit's trail but there was no residual track to follow. Nothing but thin air.

The knock at the door startled her. No one ever knocked on Billie's door. Getting to her feet, her hope leapt to the thought of Kaitlin. Maybe she had made her way here. She unlatched the door and pulled it open.

Mockler stood in her doorway. He smiled. "Hi."

Billie froze, caught off guard by his appearance. She had a crazy notion to simply close the door. She fumbled out a shaky greeting. "Hey."

"I'm sorry to bother you at home," he said. "Do you have a minute?"

She went flush. The apartment was a mess but he was standing right there and there was no way out of it without being rude. "Sure."

"Thanks."

She stepped aside and Mockler crossed into the living room and looked the place over. Her cheeks burned at the state of her flat. What was he doing here?

"Uh, can I get you anything?" She remembered the empty refrigerator and clocked the last beer she had on the coffee table. "I have, uhm, half a beer?"

"I'm fine, thanks." He scanned through the books on a shelf. "I hope we didn't spook you too bad the other night."

Her back went up. "Spook me?"

"At the station. Sorry you had to go through that. Protocol can be a pain in the butt."

"No big deal," she said, easing her guard back down. Her hand went up to emphasize a point. "Although, your partner is a real dick."

He laughed. "Odinbeck? He's a charmer, isn't he?"

Billie stuck her hands in her pockets, suddenly unsure of what to do with them. His presence made her feel awkward in her own home. "So. How have you been?"

"Stuck," he said.

"Stuck?"

"The body you found. All the weirdo stuff in that house." Mockler scratched his chin. "I'm stuck with it."

"Oh," she said. This is a business call, she realized. Why would she think anything else? "Did you identify the body?"

"Nope. I don't think we ever will." He looked at the floor. "So, I got nothing. Everything has fizzled out."

"Sounds frustrating."

"That's why I'm here." Mockler straightened up and sought out her eyes. "Would you take a walk with me? Through that house again?"

Her back stiffened. Why there? Why not just a walk down James Street or along the waterfront or the park? Anywhere but that awful place and she'd agree immediately. Her hands slipped out from her pockets and she fussed her hair, scratched her nose, straightened the hem of her shirt.

"I know it's a lot to ask," he said. "If you're not comfortable with it, just say no."

"I dunno. It didn't go too well last time."

"Yeah." He nodded his head, recalling the incident. "You kinda freaked me out last time. But that was my issue. The info you provided helped."

She looked down at her shoes. "I thought you didn't believe in this stuff?"

"I don't."

She studied his face for a moment. The abilities she possessed had nothing to do with telepathy or mind-reading. She often had difficulty sensing beguile or deceit in others but with Mockler it was different. His face, for whatever reason, was an open book to her and the trouble there was plain to read. "It's that bad, huh?"

He nodded again. "Something bad happened in that place, Billie. I need to figure it out."

"I see."

The open book policy was a two-way street and the reluctance on Billie's face was plain enough. Mockler straightened up and took a step toward the door. "I shouldn't have bothered you with this. You went through enough already in that house. I just need to work harder."

A tug of panic ripped at her as he made his exit. Now that he was here, she didn't want him to go. "Wait," she said. "I'll do it."

"I shouldn't have asked. I'm sorry. No one in their right mind would want to go back there."

"Ray," she said, "I'll do it."

He studied her face for a moment before saying anything. "You sure?"

No. Not in the least.

"Let me get my jacket."

CHAPTER 10

THE YELLOW POLICE tape was still strung over the entrance to the house on Laguna Road, like something out of a TV show. Mockler pulled the car onto the dead grass, killed the engine and looked at Billie. "You sure? We can turn around and go home."

"I'm sure." She didn't look at him, knowing he'd detect the lie if he saw her face. It would be silly to turn back now. "Just give me a second, okay?"

"Whatever you need."

The engine ticked as it cooled and Billie stalled for time. She didn't want to open up but if she was going to help Mockler, she had to make herself open to the dead. It was like relaxing a clenched muscle. She took a breath and gripped the door handle. "Okay."

She expected an onslaught of emotion as she stepped out of the car but there was nothing. The old house loomed over her, as if sulking, determined to keep its secrets to itself. The air was colder here, halfway up the mountain.

Mockler walked through the grass past the side entrance they had used earlier. "The tech guys said the generator was still set up. Ah." The metal frame of the generator flared up in the beam of his flashlight. Mockler turned the key, gave the cord a sharp yank and the engine roared up. The windows of the atrium glowed with light. "We're in business."

Billie watched him snap the yellow tape from the entrance and pass through. She took a breath, letting her heart open all the way, and followed him inside. Two paces onto the cracked marble floor and she faltered.

"You all right?" He moved in quick to prop her up.

"Yeah. I just don't like it here." Before he could offer to take her home again, she held up a hand. "I'm okay. Just saying, this is a bad place."

His eyes narrowed at her, trying to understand. "How so? I mean, how do you know that?"

"There's a lot of dead people here. A lot of sadness and misery. They're everywhere."

"And you can see them?"

She nodded. "Not all of them. Some I just feel."

Floodlights were set up along the corridor, strings of cable snaking over the floor. He led the way. "So tell me what you see. Or feel."

"There's a woman here. She owns the place. Or she did. She doesn't like all these other people here."

"Who is she? What's her name?"

Billie picked her way through the debris behind him. "She won't say. Most of them never do."

He seemed surprised at that. "They don't want you to know?"

"It's more like their old names don't matter anymore. Not where they are now."

"I see. So they don't have identities anymore?"

"They know who they are. But the names they had were like artificial things. They didn't stick after they were dead." She watched his brow furrow, the natural skepticism running deep but conflicted now. He was taking it in, trying to square it with everything his gut was probably telling him was wrong. "This sounds crazy to you, doesn't it?"

"A little." He shrugged. "Hard to get my head around, ya know? But I'm trying."

"I know you are."

He watched her hands move. Constantly in motion, rubbing the palms together or one kneading the knuckles of the other. "Are you cold?" he asked.

"No. Why?"

"Nothing." They tacked left around a corner and came to the cellar door. He pulled it open. "You still okay with this?"

"Yup." Her hand-rubbing notched up a degree and she nodded at the door. "You first."

"Watch out for the cable," he said, pointing out the heavy electrical cord running down the basement steps.

Billie followed him down and her hands shot up to cup her ears. It was like someone cranked the volume up.

"What is it?" he said.

"There's a lot more of them down here," she said. "They're all hollering at me."

He stopped. "Is it too much?"

"No." His grip on her elbow jolted her for a heartbeat. "It's just loud. Some of them want to tell me their tragedies. Others want me to leave."

She tugged her elbow to get him to let go but he didn't. His eyes zeroed in on hers. "Is this dangerous? Can they hurt you?"

"Not yet."

"What does that mean? You're not sure?" He prodded her back up the steps.

"I'm fine. Honest."

His concern for her safety set off some kind of alarm bell. It rang and rang and it wouldn't stop and his hand on her elbow confused her. Or her reaction, to be more accurate, was the confusing part. What alarmed her, Billie realized, was how much he got under her skin. She barely knew the man. This was as about as close as they had gotten but it reverberated through her like a jolt. It was like cracking a bat against a baseball at the wrong angle. The vibration stung all the way up her arm.

"Tell me about this woman you see," he said. "What does she look like?"

"She's in her thirties, maybe. And the way she's dressed,

looks like the twenties. Sort of flapperish."

Mockler swept his light over the immense cellar as if looking for the woman in question. "What else?"

"She's angry. She's always bickering with this other man. He stays hidden. I think it was her husband."

"What's she angry about?"

"She feels trapped here. And she's furious with all these other people in her house. Dead people, I mean. She wants them gone." Billie followed the detective along, side-stepping the debris on the floor. "She did something bad."

He stopped. "What did she do?"

Billie rubbed her hands together. "I can't tell. She's hiding it from me. She knows I can see her now and she's pissed."

"Are you cold?"

"No. Why?"

He nodded at her restless hands. "You've been rubbing your hands like that since we stepped inside."

"I do that a lot," she confessed. "When I see them. It's like a nervous tick."

"Right. Say the word and we can leave. Deal?"

She looked around the tangle of old furniture and boxes scattered around the floor. "I need to sit down for a second."

Mockler flipped an apple crate over and pulled it close. Billie dropped onto it, clutching her stomach. He squatted down, eye level with her. "What's happening now?"

"I feel sick," Billie said. "It's the woman. She's trying to drive me away."

A cold tingle traced up his spine. "They can do that?"

"Some. Powerful ones. She's a piece of work this one. She keeps trying to squeeze my heart." Billie snapped her head to the left as if hearing something. Her eyes narrowed. "But she slipped up. I saw something about her. I think she killed someone."

"How?"

"I dunno. I just got a flash of a knife. A really big one, like a machete or something. And a lot of blood." Billie squinted into the dark. "It's gone now, but it was like there was a purpose to it. It wasn't done out of anger or self-defence. I don't understand."

Mockler studied her face as she spoke, noting the looks of shock or recoil that played over it as if she was witnessing the crime firsthand. Like most people in his line of work, he had a finely tuned radar for liars and bullshitters. Billie was reacting physically to something that he couldn't see or hear. It was difficult to maintain his poker face.

Then her breath cut short.

"What is it?"

"She was up to something bad," Billie whispered. "Like occult stuff. Dark magic. I don't know how else to describe it. The killing had something to do with that."

Watching her shiver, he put his hand on her arm. It was all he could think of to calm her. She flinched.

"This is gonna sound crazy but it was part of some ritual. Like a spell or something." Billie looked down and was surprised to see her hand covering his. As if caught, he was about to pull away but she gripped his hand tighter to hold it still.

Don't go.

"Do you want to leave?"

"I'm okay. She's gone now. She doesn't want me to see anymore." Billie patted his knuckles once before his hand slipped away, the moment gone. "What do you know about this place?"

"I'll tell you in a minute," he said. "If you're up for it, I want to know more about what you see."

She held out her hand and he tugged her up to her feet.

"Is it always like that?" he asked. "The physical reaction?"

She nodded. "Sometimes I feel the trauma they went through."

"Could they ever hurt you? Like in a serious way?"

"I don't know. I've gotten sick from it before but nothing serious." She shook off the last of the nausea and steadied herself. "Can I ask you something?"

"Anything."

"Do you believe any of this or do you think it's crazy?"

He scratched his chin. "It's hard to get my head around it, you know?"

"It is," Billie agreed. "I never used to believe it either."

They went on, winding through the trash and broken furniture of the dim cellar. Only one bank of floodlights had been left in the basement, its light glowing through the doorway to the farthest chamber. Mockler aimed the flashlight through the pathway ahead.

"Watch the broken glass there," he said. "Do you know what happened to the woman you saw?"

"She died. But not here, somewhere else. I got a glimpse of an institution or a hospital. I think she went crazy."

He looked at her sharply, as if startled.

"What?"

"Nothing," he said and went on. "What else?"

"There's a lot of other people here. Some of them want to leave but they can't."

"What's stopping them?"

"I can't tell. Some of them died in the house and now they're trapped here. Others were drawn here after they died." Billie ducked her head under a low-hanging pipe. "It has to do with the woman who owned the house. Like she caused it."

"These other people who died here. Can you see any of them?"

"There's a man who's covered in blood. He's young. Looks like a hippie, long hair and a beard. He died down here in the basement."

"How did he die?"

"He says he was murdered. I'm getting this awful pain in my neck. I think his throat was cut."

Again, Mockler stopped and looked at her. "Who killed him?"

"He doesn't want to say," Billie said. "There was a group of people involved. But he's still afraid of them and doesn't want to say anymore."

"Do you know when this happened?"

Billie skewed her lips, trying to think. "Early seventies? The hippie era."

Passing under the arched doorway, the basement opened up into a larger chamber lit up by the bank of portable lights. The caved-in pit in the centre of the floor yawned open, emptied of its awful secret.

"This is where all the bad stuff happened," she said. Billie shivered as a cold wave passed over her. When she looked up, she clocked the detective scrutinizing her. "What is it?"

"What do you know about this place?"

Billie shrugged. "Nothing. It's a haunted house, that's it. Why?"

"I looked into the background of this property," he said. "And you've just described what happened in this house."

CHAPTER 11

"THE HOUSE WAS built back in nineteen eighteen by a man named Edward James Bourdain. He built it for his new bride, Evelyn Francis."

Mockler reached into a pocket and produced a handful of photographs. He held one out to Billie. An old tintype of a bearded man in a cravat standing behind a much younger woman seated in a chair. Both appeared stiff and formal but there was a light to the woman's eyes.

"She was young," Billie said.

"Eighteen when she married," Mockler confirmed. "He was forty-six. Bourdain inherited the textiles mills of his father and then went on to make his own fortune in ironworks. Evelyn Francis was a blue blood of the local gentry. This house was his wedding present to her."

Water dripped somewhere in the cellar, it's tap-tap echoing around them.

Billie gazed at the photograph, entranced by its image. "This is her. The woman who's still in the house."

"Are you sure?"

"Positive. There's no faking those eyes of hers." She flapped the photo in her hand. "She's the one who messed with things she shouldn't have. So was he, but he was a dabbler. She embraced it."

"Right on the nose," Mockler said. "Bourdain was into all kinds of stuff, mysticism and witchcraft and weirdo philosophies. He got her into it but Evelyn apparently fell hard for the occult stuff. She gained quite a reputation for it too."

Billie steadied herself. Stepping into the chamber brought a fresh wave of nausea. "What happened to her?"

"There was a police investigation after one of their maids disappeared. There were rumours that Evelyn had murdered her in a bizarre ritual but she was never charged. There was no body, so no charges were ever laid."

Billie knelt down and placed her palm flat on the floor. Her eyes closed and then after a moment, she opened them again. "She was murdered. In this room."

"Do you see her?"

"Just flashes, nothing definite. There were other deaths too. A lot of blood has been spilt down here." She straightened up and brushed the dust from her hands. "What happened to the owners?"

"Things went downhill after that. The stock market crash

wiped them out and the two of them became recluses in the house. Then she killed her husband. He was found down here with his throat cut."

Billie covered her ears with her hands. "Ooh. She doesn't like that."

"Who doesn't like it?"

"Her, Evelyn. She doesn't like us talking about killing her husband. She started shrieking at me."

"She's back?"

"She never left," Billie said. Her face winced, as if in pain. "She's screaming at me that it's all lies and slander."

Mockler looked over the room. He didn't necessarily want to see anything but he couldn't stop himself from looking. "Where is she?"

"Right beside you. Screaming into your ear."

Mockler flinched and backed away, the way one does when a wasp flies too close. There was nothing there. "Can you tell her to get lost?"

"She won't listen to me." Billie looked at the photograph again. "What happened to her?"

Mockler shook off the clammy sensation crawling up his spine and went on. "She was locked up in Hamilton Asylum. Killed by another inmate in nineteen thirty-seven."

"That did it. She's gone." Billie tracked something across the room. "What happened to the house after that?"

"It sat empty for a while before being purchased by this

man." He held out another photograph. "Howard Gunther Albee. A writer during the pulp era. He wrote spooky books and stuff. Like the owners, a devotee of the occult."

Billie studied the man in the photograph. A broad face with small eyes hidden behind wire-rimmed spectacles. "Was he famous?"

"Not that I know of," Mockler replied. "Have you seen him in the house?"

The man in the photo was a stranger to her. "No. What happened to him?"

"He disappeared. After a prolonged absence, a colleague came to check on him but he had vanished. All of his stuff was still here, the suitcases and whatnot. There was even a half-written page in the typewriter but Albee himself was gone."

"He was never found?"

"Nope. Gone without a trace. But the police found blood down here in the basement." Mockler nodded at the broken cavity in the floor. "Right in that spot, actually."

Billie's eyes widened at that. "So was that him, Albee? The body in the pit?"

"That's what I thought too but it's not him. The coroner said the body you found was a couple decades old. Albee disappeared in forty-three." Mockler shuffled through the photographs in his hand. "Here's where it gets weirder."

"Like it's not weird enough?" Billie joked.

"When Bourdain, the original owner, was found dead in this

space, the walls and floors were painted with weirdo symbols. Pentagrams and witchcraft stuff. Evelyn had apparently been the artist who had done it. Now, all of that had been scrubbed off and painted over when the house was put up for sale again in nineteen thirty-one. When the police came back in forty-three looking for the missing writer, Albee, the symbols were back. Take a look."

Billie took the photo he held out. An overhead angle of the basement floor, painted with an elaborate pentagram with candles set into the five points. In the centre of the star was a large puddle of dark blood. Billie scanned the floor before her with the crude symbol painted there and compared it to the one in the photograph. "It's the same one."

"Yup," he said. He pointed at the floor. "What you're looking at here is actually the fourth occurrence of this symbol."

"Fourth?"

"That we know of," he explained. "Now, there are no photos of the original pentagram that Evelyn painted but I imagine it looked like this. After it was scrubbed off, it shows up again with Albee's disappearance. Again, it's scrubbed off at the time. It shows up a third time a few decades later with the death of this man."

He handed over two more photographs. Billie gazed down at a picture of another pentagram on the floor. It was identical to the other photograph, the only difference being the police office in the picture revealed a more recent era. The second photograph was a mug shot of a young man with long hair and a scraggly beard. Billie felt her throat catch at the familiarity of the face. "This is the man I saw. The hippie."

"Stanley Whistler," Mockler reported. "Draft dodger from Ohio relocated here. Found dead in October of seventy-two. Guess where he was found?"

Her eyes dropped automatically to the caved-in pit in the floor. "Here too."

"Yup. Right in the same spot. Another pentagram on the floor, which you can see in the photo there."

"He was cut open," she said. "Like an animal."

"That's right. His throat was slashed then his belly was cut open. According to the notes, his insides were spread across the room."

She tried to block the image from her mind but once Mockler had said it, she could see it as plain as day. The body on the floor, mangled and brutalized. His intestines unspooled like cords of rope across the cement floor. "Was anyone arrested for the murder?"

"No. The detectives at the time had little to go on. Whistler was a drifter with no ties here, no real friends. The only leads they had was this group of hippie people that Whistler had been seen with. Apparently, these people were modern-day witches or something but the police couldn't find any of them. They must have fled town after the murder."

"Witches?"

"The reports were contradictory. They were described as hippies, flower children, witches and-or Satanists."

"And they re-painted the same pentagram and stuff on the walls?"

"Yup." Mockler took the photos back. "Do you see anything about this Stanley kid? Or what happened to him?"

"A tiny bit. But it's foggy. Residual energy."

He raised an eyebrow. "Residual?"

"It's like an echo of a traumatic event. I had a glimpse of him being held down. There was someone wearing a robe but their face is hidden."

"A robe?"

"Like a costume cape or something. There was some kind of ritual going on."

Mockler scratched his stubble, mulling it over. "Just like Evelyn Bourdain, crazy spells and stuff?"

"I guess so." Billie paced forward until the toes of her shoes touched the outer edge of the painted circle. "So this pentagram is the fourth occurrence?"

"That we know of. The place has been empty for so long, there may have been other incidents that we just don't know about."

Billie toed the paint on the floor, scuffing it with her shoe. It flaked away like dry sand.

"I wouldn't do that," he said. "It's dried blood."

She jerked backward. "Eeew. Are you serious?"

"Pig's blood. According to the lab."

Billie retraced her steps. It was silly but she felt safer being within arm's reach of him. "Can I ask you something?"

"Anything."

"What do you think is going on here?"

He scratched his chin for a long time before answering. "I think it's like a self-fulfilling prophecy. The house is rumoured to be haunted, all kinds of stories and folk tales floating around about what happened here. That attracts its own bad business. People looking to do something bad come here because of its reputation. It's like a loop. The myth attracts bad things, the bad things propel the myth. And on and on."

It was a cop's take. A method of breaking down all the rampant, contradictory details to get at the problem itself. She chewed on it, seeing the logic of it. "Makes sense," she concluded.

"There's been an uptick in this stuff," he said, nodding to the glyphs on the walls. "Crimes with some kind of devil-worship connection. At first, I thought it had something to do with your friend Gantry but I'm not sure. I think something else is going on."

Billie clammed up at the mention of that name. Gantry was just trouble.

"Have you heard from him?" Mockler asked.

"No. Last I heard he was back in England." John Gantry was a bit of a sore point between them. The slippery Englishman seemed to be a sore between everyone who knew him. Gantry was the one who had helped Billie understand her abilities. Detective Mockler, on the other hand, was after the man for suspicion of murder.

"I heard that too. I also heard he was incinerated in a factory explosion in Oslo." Mockler shrugged. "I got my fingers crossed that rumour is true."

"I heard it was a church fire."

The sound of water dripping echoed from a dark corner.

Mockler looked up at her. "Your turn." He smiled as he said this. "I want to know what you think is going on here. Why is this place home to so much misery?"

"You're not gonna like my answer." It was as honest as she could be.

"Try me. I'm open to anything at this point."

She took a moment, trying to find a way to phrase her answer so it didn't sound so crazy to him. There wasn't one. "This Evelyn woman? She was playing around with something she shouldn't have. And she summoned something bad into this place and it's been here ever since. It draws people to it, like a magnet. And bad things happen."

Silence crept across the room, leaving her response to simply hang there in the air as the detective pondered it. Unlike herself, Billie noted his poker face. It was stone.

Finally, he looked at her. "What is it? Like a ghost?"

"I don't know what to call it." She folded her arms over her stomach as if she'd eaten something bad. "It's not a ghost. It was never alive to begin with. It's old and it's evil to the core. And all it wants to do is hurt people. Or make people hurt others."

"Hey," he said, taking a step closer. "You okay? You look a little green."

"It doesn't like me talking about it." Billie wiped her forearm across her brow to dry the cold sweat blooming quickly. "And it's getting close."

Mockler didn't believe in any of this stuff but that did nothing to settle the prickle of gooseflesh on the back of his neck. "It's in the room?"

"I have to leave," she said. Then, like a puppet with its strings cut, Billie collapsed in a heap and threw up all over the floor.

CHAPTER 12

"JUST COME OVER," Tammy said into the phone. "It's been ages. We'll just hang out."

She listened to the man on the other end blather on. Jay was a friend. A hook-up initially but later a friend. He was a film editor and they often moved in the same circles. More than a few times, they had been each other's last minute dates for functions that required a partner. At the moment, he was being a pain.

"No, Jay." Tammy rolled her eyes as she corrected his assumption. "It's not a booty call. I just don't want to be alone right now."

Another spew of blather down the line. Tammy waited for a break in the chatter. "I'm just working and it's tedious and, I don't know... Do you have something better to do?"

Blather, blather, excuse, excuse.

"Fine," she finally said. "Be that way." She hung up and tossed her phone down.

Hunkered down at her desk, Tammy had set aside the evening to tweak a set of photographs she had taken for Jen's shop. Jen had an article coming out in a magazine and had asked Tammy to do the pics. The shoot had gone well and a good batch of the photos had turned out but she wanted to tweak them further. All the ladies were there but some weirdo tension was brewing between Billie and Jen. The two of them had known each other since high school and there was plenty of history there to dig at them both. Tammy stayed out of it, leaving them to sort it out.

Sitting down to work, Tammy found her motivation dwindled quickly as the exhaustion set in. She had barely slept the last two nights because of the nightmares and the fiasco at the abandoned house. The other stuff she had initially dismissed as exhaustion but the weirdo factor kept edging up and she was having difficulty dispelling it all. The sound of footsteps in the other room, the sense of dread that had settled over her apartment, the startling voice in her ear that had made her jump out of her skin.

That had been the prompt to call Jay. The creepiness was edging up her nerves and she simply didn't want to be alone. Jay had nixed that idea, moaning about how bored he would be watching her work. Douche.

Tammy lingered at her laptop, forcing herself to concentrate on the fine-tuning she needed to apply to the photos. Unable to shake the creeping sensation that she was being watched, she sat with her back to the wall. She had read once that gunfighters in the Old West sat this way, to avoid being shot in the back by some brazen coward.

She wished she had a gun. Or a gunfighter, to sit and keep watch.

She couldn't stop thinking about what Billie had said earlier. Tammy learned of her friend's talents the night that she and Jen and Kaitlin had confronted Billie about her withdrawal from the world. It had been a half-assed intervention which Billie shut down by informing the trio that she could talk to ghosts. The ladies' reaction had been mixed. Kaitlin believed without question. Jen refused to hear another word. Tammy was in the middle somewhere but leaning more toward Jen than Kaitlin. It seemed crazy but in the two months since that time, she had seen things that had eaten away at her resistance to the idea. Any vestige of doubt had crumbled after the visit to the murder house. Kaitlin's odd behaviour and sudden disappearance had only underscored it all. And something Billie had said earlier kept nagging at her; the idea that something from that creepy house had followed Kaitlin home.

Could it have followed her home too? Was that the reason behind the strange sounds and unearthly whisper in her ear? Or was it all in her head? Was it too much to ask of Jay to get off his butt and come keep her company when she needed it?

"You're overtired," she said aloud. "Go to bed."

Ignoring her own advice, she scrolled through photograph after photograph from Jen's shoot, liking some and dismissing others. Something seemed off. She scrolled back and popped one picture into a new window.

A nice shot of Jen, Billie, and Kaitlin smiling for the camera. Their signature mugs all around. Jen's smile was full and bright where Billie's came off as lopsided, as if smiling came unnaturally to her. Kaitlin normally had a huge smile, all teeth and eyes curled into crescents but not in this photo. Kaitlin's whole face was foggy and pixelated, as if someone had used the smudge tool in the photo editor to blur her face.

Tammy winced, thinking she had messed up the shot in-camera. She flicked the image away and brought up the next one in the file. A duplicate of the first snapped a second or two later. Same smiles, same blurry vision of Kaitlin's face.

Something cold fluttered down in Tammy's belly.

She pored through the rest of the photographs. Every photo of Kaitlin's face was pixelated into obscurity. It was as if someone had gone through Tammy's photo set with a vengeance, eager to mar every snap of the young woman's face.

It wasn't a glitch in the camera and it wasn't a problem with the lighting. Everyone else in the photographs looked fine. Only Kaitlin had been singled out and defaced.

Tammy killed the program and closed the laptop. This was no mistake. It was deliberate. Something bad had targeted her friend and now Kaitlin had disappeared. Snatching up the phone, Tammy crossed into the living room and dialed another number. She prayed that Billie would pick up.

CHAPTER 13

THE TIRES SPIT gravel across the steps as Mockler stomped the gas pedal to get away from the Murder House. Billie lay flat across the backseat where he had all but thrown her in his haste to get out of there. The police tape stretched across the driveway flashed up in the headlights and snapped as he gunned through it.

"Billie!" He twisted around to look at her but all he could see were her legs. "You okay back there?"

No response. The car fishtailed across the gravel as it swung onto the main road, almost swerving into the ditch on the far side. The road was dark and, luckily, devoid of traffic.

He was still numb from what he had witnessed, even with all of the spooky business he had heard so far. After Billie had collapsed and vomited all over the floor, he ran to help her but she had slipped out of his fingers at the last second. She had been pulled away, sliding across the cement floor at a brisk pace as if dragged by some unseen force. The look of absolute terror in her eyes had frozen his blood as she slid clear across the floor and straight toward the open pit in the centre of the pentagram. Whatever force had taken hold of her meant to throw her down into the crater.

Billie's fingernails had clawed across the concrete as she tried to latch onto something and the awful sound of it had snapped him out of his paralysis. He bolted and tackled Billie before she was flung into the pit. Worst of all was the reality-splitting tug-of-war that ensued with whatever unseen thing that gripped the young woman's leg. Billie became a wishbone, split down the middle and pulled apart. His grip on her wrist was slipping but in the end, Billie had saved herself, shrieking at the invisible thing to go away and kicking at it in a frenzy.

The tension slacked and she tumbled onto him. Yanking Billie to her feet, he rushed the woman out of that awful place.

Murder House. More like hell house, he thought.

"Ray?" Her voice drifted up from the backseat.

Mockler hit the brakes and skidded the vehicle onto the shoulder. "Billie? Are you okay?"

Throwing the car into park, he launched out of the driver's seat and as rushed into the back. Billie propped herself onto her elbows. Her hair draped down over her face, hiding her features. He slid in next to her, leaving the door open to keep the dome light on.

"Easy," he said.

Her hand trembled as it rose to shield her eyes from the

overhead light. "Turn it off," she rasped.

The car went dark as he shut the door and he felt her collapse onto him. "Are you hurt?" he asked. "Talk to me."

"I'm okay now." Her voice was fragile and weak. "It's passing."

He couldn't see any detail inside the darkened car, just her outline. "I can't tell if you're injured or not."

"I'm fine. I just need a minute."

They sat there in the dim glow of the dashboard lights and he listened to her breathing. His own pulse calmed when he felt her head fall onto his shoulder. He didn't want to stir or disrupt the moment. The sudden sense of peace was strange, a stark contrast to the appalling nightmare they had just fled in the old house.

"Thanks for getting us out of there," she said.

He didn't respond, didn't move a muscle.

She tilted her eyes up. "What's wrong?"

Mockler exhaled. He hadn't realized that he had been holding his breath the whole time. "That," he whispered, "was the craziest thing I've ever seen."

"Welcome to my world."

He didn't find it very funny. "Billie, what the hell just happened?"

It hurt to shrug. "I don't know. It wanted to drag me into the pit."

"What did? What was it?"

"I don't know how to describe it. Not without sounding

completely insane to you."

"Try me."

Billie tried to look at her fingers but it was too dark. The tips of them stung, scraped raw along the floor. "It was the woman. The one who murdered her husband."

He felt his pulse tick back up the scale. "This is what you see? This is what you have to go through?"

"Not always. This was something else." Her ear was squished flat against his shoulder but she didn't want to move just yet. She didn't want to talk about this right now either. "Were you hurt?"

"Me? No. I think my heart stopped for a full minute. But that's all."

He stirred and, out of the blue, she felt his hand settle atop hers. It felt warm and safe and it sparked a jolt right through her. This was getting dangerous, she thought. This was trouble. Pull back. Despite the warning blips going off in her brain, she didn't move. Just the opposite, she had the odd sensation of melting.

"Billie," he hushed. "I saw you dragged across the floor. But right now, away from that awful place, I still can't believe it."

She wished he would just stop talking. She wanted to just sit here in the dark and draw out the moment and, she mused, pretend for a little while that the car was actually a little boat drifting out to sea with just the two of them.

"Don't think about it," she suggested. "It will drive you crazy."

"How can I not think about it? I feel like the rug's been

pulled out from under me."

His grip locked harder onto her hand. It almost hurt and she wanted him to squeeze harder. "It'll wear off," Billie said. "In a few days, it'll seem like it never happened. Ow."

He felt her flinch and realized too late that he had been crushing her hand. "I'm sorry."

Her hand cooled as his lifted away. "Don't let go," she whispered.

His hand returned and this time the electric charge jolted both ways, each able to decipher the pulse of the other.

Trouble came when she tilted up to look at him and saw his face in the glow of the dash. His focus locked onto hers and it held there for what seemed to be a lifetime, neither of them knowing where to go to next. Tortuous indecision and tingly expectation. The nigh unbearable moments before a first kiss.

This was all she had thought about. This pristine moment. Two months, she had pondered and dreamt and fretted and despaired over it. And now, somehow, it was actually going to happen.

She flinched and recoiled, her right hand pushing his chest to break his momentum.

"Stop."

"What's wrong?"

Her hand covered her mouth. "I just threw up."

The look in his eyes shifted into confusion. "Oh. Right."

She slid away as the cold slither of self-consciousness chilled her. "Oh, God. That would have been disgusting."

He opened his mouth to say something but nothing came out. The moment passed from suddenly awkward to ludicrous and then he laughed. "Right. I kinda forgot that."

One trickle of laughter is infectious and her clammy embarrassment tilted into the farce of it all. "Me too."

"I guess that woulda been, uh, unpleasant, huh?"

"And wrong," she added. "We can't do that."

The moment, whatever it had been, vaporized into thin air. Both of them sobered quickly in the non-afterglow of an almost moment.

Mockler rubbed his eyes as if shaking it off. "I'm sorry," he said. "I don't know what came over me."

"Yeah," she lied. "Me neither."

Silence crept in as each settled into their separate ends of the backseat like boxers retreating to their corners. The kiss that had never happened had, nonetheless, left a bad taste in the mouth.

"You all right," he asked, for what seemed the hundredth time that night.

"Peachy," she lied again.

"Okay." His hands raised up as if throwing in the towel. He reached for the door handle. "Let's get out of here."

"Sure."

The car dipped a little as he swung out of the backseat and dipped again when he dropped under the wheel. Billie scrambled her brains for something, anything, to say but Mockler turned the ignition and slid the transmission into gear. He swung back onto the road and drove without another word and Billie fumed in the backseat, hating every minute of the awkward drive home.

That moment, that tiny sliver of time and space that she had envisioned so many times had crashed on the rocks and gone belly-up in the worst possible way.

And now it was gone.

Forever.

Was it possible to die from undiluted mortification? If it was, then Billie predicted that she had about ten seconds to live before the end came.

CHAPTER 14

KYLE DROPPED ONTO the sofa, feeling the weight of the day settle over him. Scrounging around for the remote seemed like too much effort so he just sat before the darkened flat screen. The last three hours had been spent circling the downtown core looking for Kaitlin. He had started at all the usual places Kaitlin frequented and then expanded his search from there, cycling through the streets to any place that Kaitlin had ever mentioned in the past, no matter how remote. His efforts had amounted to a big fat zero. No one had seen his girlfriend in two days.

Coasting home on the bike, he had kept his fingers crossed that he would walk into their apartment and find his missing girlfriend safely ensconced on the sofa with a bowl of popcorn and a perfectly reasonable explanation for her strange disappearance. That hope evaporated the moment he walked in the door and found the place in the same state that he had left it. Empty.

His eyes grew heavier by the moment and he dug for one last ounce of strength to propel himself into the bedroom. Then he heard the door click open.

"Hello?" he muttered, sitting up.

Kaitlin stood in the foyer.

Kyle shot to his feet. "Kaitlin? Where have you been?"

He rushed to her but stopped short. Something wasn't right. His girlfriend's clothes were muddied and torn, her hair a tangled mess. Kaitlin looked as if she had run an obstacle course. She remained still and her eyes looked over the apartment like she didn't recognize the place.

"What happened to you?" Her arms and hands were red with scratch marks as if she'd clawed her way through a thorn bush. "Are you hurt?"

Kaitlin's eyes were glassy, almost drugged, and she had yet to even look at him. "Don't touch me," she said.

"I've been looking everywhere for you. Where did you go?"

"Out," she mumbled and moved past him.

She had lost her shoes somewhere. Her bare feet left muddy footprints on the tile floor as she drifted into the living room.

Kyle stammered for a moment, unsure of what to do. A hundred different scenarios raced through his head, trying to understand what had happened to her. She had been abducted. Or she had been rufied at a bar and was still feeling the drug's effect. He followed her into the living room. "Maybe we should go to the hospital."

Kaitlin rummaged through the mess on the coffee table. "Where is it?" she hissed.

"Where's what?"

"The board!" She hurled the pillows from the sofa, plunged her hand between the cushions.

"What are you talking about?" Kyle took her by the arm. "Stop it. Let's get a cab, go the hospital—"

"Get your hands off me!" She shoved him away and then dropped to her knees to peer under the sofa. "What did you do with it?"

"What? Your fucking voodoo board? I didn't do anything with it!"

"Don't lie to me." She turned to the bookcase and tossed book after book to the floor.

"It's gone."

"Gone?" The look in her eye had gone from dim to manic. "Gone where?"

"Billie took it," he said. "She and Tammy came looking for you."

The fury came fast. "That bitch. Why did she take it? It doesn't belong to her."

"She said you shouldn't be messing with that stuff."

"That stupid bitch!" Kaitlin's arms dropped and the fire within her seemed to go out. "She thinks she knows everything. She doesn't know shit."

He approached her again but cautiously, the way one would a

wild animal. "Sit down, honey. You need to calm down. Tell me what happened."

Kaitlin lowered herself slowly into the armchair. Books and knick-knacks were scattered around her dirty feet and a faraway look returned to her eyes. "I made a friend," she said quietly.

He leaned in, warning signals flashing at the mention of a "friend". The person responsible for her disappearance. "What friend? Who is he?"

"She."

"Okay," he spoke slowly. "Who is she?"

"She's lonely," Kaitlin said. "She's going to come and stay with us now."

The notion sent a creep up his spine. "Who, Kaitlin? What's her name?"

"Evelyn."

"Evelyn who?"

Kaitlin folded her hands in her lap. "She doesn't like it where she is now. She wants to leave."

He'd heard enough. It was time to call the police. He should have called them the second she walked in the door. Kyle patted his pockets but his phone wasn't there. "Kaitlin, did this woman take you somewhere? Did she give you something?"

"She did. She's very generous."

Kyle patted down the sofa for his phone. It must have slipped out of his pocket. "What did she give you, honey? Was it a drug? Booze?"

"She's here," Kaitlin whispered.

"What?"

"She's coming up the steps now."

His blood ran cold when he heard the noise from the corridor. Footsteps out in the hallway. Kyle was already scared. Now he was outright terrified.

A thin smile creased Kaitlin's face. "She brought her friends too."

There was a click as the doorknob turned and then the apartment door creaked open. Kyle was only slightly aware of the warm sensation spreading through his crotch as his bladder let go.

CHAPTER 15

ONE LONELY WINDOW was lit when Mockler pulled into his driveway and killed the engine. Going up the eroded porch steps, he looked at his watch and wondered if Christina was home yet. There was little point in wondering, she kept her own hours these days.

Hitting the switch-plate in the kitchen, he dropped his keys and his ID into the bowl on the counter. Then he remembered the sidearm clipped on his belt. It was unusual for him to bring it home. He almost always left it at the precinct, preferring not to have it in the house. Hell, he didn't even like wearing the damn thing but his sergeant had chewed him out the last time she caught him without it. He opened a cupboard and reached up, slipping the weapon into a bowl on the topmost shelf where the fancier dishes were kept. Out of sight and out of mind.

Scrounging a beer from the fridge, he leaned back against the counter and tried not to let the sight of his own house depress him. There was a stack of packed cardboard boxes on the floor and another on a kitchen chair. The table was cluttered with glassware and the crumpled newspaper used to pack it in. A cupboard door stood open, the shelves within half-empty. It was a sad sight.

Most of the house was in the same sorry state; packing boxes cluttering the floors, pictures taken down, items swaddled in newspaper. A home interrupted and put on hold. He hated it, the disruption it caused and the sense of instability. Mockler passed through the chaos of the living room and moved on through to the sunroom at the back of the house but he couldn't escape the packing material or empty spaces. Change was happening and he didn't like it and there was no refuge from it. He kept moving, pushing out the back door to the yard.

Here, at least, there were no signs of disruption. Just a backyard that needed to be cleaned up now that autumn was here. The patio table was covered with dead leaves and the barbecue needed to be covered up. Mockler eased down onto the step and sipped his beer, grimacing over the fact that the only comfortable spot in the house was outside of it.

The past few months had seen such a sea change in a house that he had once had such hopes for. The pall that he and Christina had lived under for so long had finally lifted. Much of it, he knew, he had brought into the house himself. Moving into the homicide unit had been a goal for a long time, one he had achieved eighteen months ago. The youngest member of the of the homicide unit in twenty years, the staff sergeant had informed him when she welcomed into the detail. It had felt good, crossing that goal line and he dove into the work, determined to earn his place on the team. To solve murders and ensure justice to the grieving and to apprehend the guilty for what they had done. That was the intent, at least, but six months into the new job, he began to question whether he was truly cut out for the work. Until then, he had always thought of himself as having thick skin, of being able to compartmentalize his life between work and home and keep the two apart. Working the homicide detail had shattered that illusion to the point where he wondered if his goal for the last decade had been a misstep all along. The misery of the job had gotten under his skin and, even worse, he was bringing it home with him. The job came with a price. The misery settled into his skin and then leeched into the home that he and Christina had made. It began to infect her as well. Christina had been prone to bouts of depression in the past but it was part of who she was and he accepted that. The bouts would last a couple days or even a week but they would eventually pass and Christina would become herself again.

A year into the new position at work, Christina had fallen under a dark cloud and hadn't come up for air again. The depression was so deep, so intractable that it scared him. Therapy hadn't helped, the couples-counselling had zero effect and his own pathetic attempts to raise her spirits fell flat. He left his sidearm at the office, afraid to bring it into the house. At times, they shuffled around like zombies, barely aware of the other. The dream home they had bought three years ago became a plague house, the two of them sick with some illness that was eating them alive. No one spoke of the wedding plans anymore.

Two months ago, something changed. Just as the humid swelter of summer was biting down, when the oppressive pall over them was at its worst, the clouds parted and the sun came out. Christina lifted out of her depression as if waking from a long sleep. His own dark thoughts and stifled heart altered also and the mood within the house brightened almost overnight. It was like throwing open the windows after a long, stultifying winter. Fresh air and sunshine brought them back to life. And, for a little while, they were happy again.

It just wasn't the same as before. While he was relieved to see the smile return to Christina's beautiful face, there was something different about it now. A wariness to her eyes, like she didn't quite recognize him anymore. Give it time, he told himself, things would go back to the way they were. That had yet to happen. A light had gone out between them and, to any observant eye, was not rekindling. They faked it for a little while but when the fall winds came and the leaves started turning red, neither of them had the stomach to keep up the charade. So a decision was made.

Compounding the problem was the question of Billie Culpepper, whom he had met in the summer when he had almost killed her in pursuit of a known criminal. He didn't know what to make of her. Their paths kept crossing and an odd friendship had sprung up. Maybe it had been the affront of knocking her into a coma when they first met that allowed them to speak plainly to one another. Maybe he felt responsible for her, or that a debt was owed. Whatever it was, he found an easy comfort in her presence and would often spill stuff that he normally kept bottled up. She, in turn, shared weird insights into her own oddball life, stuff she also seemed to keep hidden from friends. It was like an odd no-bullshit zone had been established after putting the poor girl in the hospital. It didn't make sense but he stopped questioning it after a while. Let it be.

What had happened earlier tonight was a different matter altogether but he wasn't sure which incident was more troubling. Almost kissing her or seeing her physically assaulted by some unseen force?

A noise from inside the house made him turn around. A light went on. He heard Christina call his name.

"Out here," he hollered.

The back door swung open. "Hey," Christina said. "What'cha doing out here?"

"I didn't want to look at the mess in there," he said.

"Not much fun to come home to, is it?"

"Nope."

Christina eased down onto the step beside him, careful not to spill the glass of wine she had poured. She tucked her hair back behind one ear and took a long sigh. As tired as she seemed, she was still radiant, still beautiful and he was grateful to see her. After the long months of depression that had worn her down over the previous year, she seemed like a completely new person.

She sipped her wine. "How was your day?"

"Long," he said. "And weird."

"Weird, huh?" Christina looked at him. "Wanna talk about it?"

The question took him aback, unused to it for so long. Over the last year, Christina's depression had been so deep that some days she could barely speak at all. It would take him forever to coax a scrap of conversation out of her. To hear the concern in her voice over himself was still relatively new. Not that it mattered much now. "Not really," he said.

They watched the leaves flutter down from the elm tree that shaded the yard, twinkling and turning in the yellow haze from the street.

"I don't think I have it in me to do any more packing tonight," she said.

"Don't worry about it."

"But there's still so much to do. And I don't want to get stuck doing it all if you get called away."

"You won't," he said. "I'll make the time. We still have the weekend too."

"God, I hate packing." Christina gave out a long sigh that drooped her shoulders. "How did we accumulate so much stuff?"

He looked back at the house. "Maybe you were right about this place. It was too big for us. Too much space to fill up."

It had been a bone of contention when they had bought the place three years ago; why the two of them would need a four bedroom house. The idea of having kids hadn't even been raised.

Recalling that long ago discussion, Christina's eyes dimmed and some of the brightness fell away. She shook her head as if trying to ward off what was coming next. She got to her feet. "Okay. I'm going to bed."

"You all right?" he asked.

"Yeah. All things considered." She opened the door but stopped before going back inside. "I tried to call you earlier but I couldn't get through."

"Oh?" He slid his phone out from his pocket. "Anything important?"

"Nah."

Mockler thumbed on his phone but it remained dark. "Ah. It's dead."

"That explains why I couldn't get through." Christina crossed into the house. "Don't stay up too late."

He watched the leafs tumble for another minute before following her inside. Plugging his phone in, he scrolled through the call list but Christina's call wasn't logged there. Nothing had been for over an hour.

Easing down onto the couch, he clicked on the news but the dead phone kept nagging at him. He couldn't help wonder if something urgent had come up while he was stuck in blackout mode.

CHAPTER 16

"THIS IS FUCKED up," Tammy blurted out, barging her way past Billie and marching straight for the kitchen.

Billie rubbed the bridge of her nose and regretted answering the knock at the door. Good news never arrives pounding on doors after sunset. "Fucked up how?"

"In the worst possible way," Tammy spat. She yanked the fridge open, bending down to inspect the contents. "I need a drink."

The refrigerator was next to bare. Billie scrounged up two glasses and opened a cupboard. A bottle of Glenfiddich came down, half full, as the optimists say. "Grab some ice," she said. "Then sit down. Explain the fucked-up part slowly."

Tammy dropped into a chair and splayed her arms across the small kitchen table. It tilted under the weight, lopsided from a faulty leg. "We never should have gone to that creepy house," Tammy said.

No kidding, Billie thought. Having just gotten home from her second trip to the Murder House, she concurred that it was nothing but trouble.

After Mockler brought her home, Billie had clattered into her apartment feeling drained and spent. Brushing her teeth twice to scour off the lingering tang of vomit, she couldn't stop her mind from analyzing every detail of her conversation with Mockler. Sure, she had seen horrific ghosts and been attacked by some dark entity but the focus of her thoughts was fixated on the homicide detective. They had almost kissed. Was it possible Mockler was attracted to her too? She already knew the answer but her brain refused to accept it, dismissing it as ludicrous and delusional. This time, her brain couldn't deny what had almost happened. Still, it spun into overdrive trying.

Ice cubes clattered over the floor as Tammy scooped ice into the glasses. Her hands were shaking badly and she finally gave up.

"Easy," Billie said. "What happened?"

"Something is in my apartment," Tammy stammered. Even her voice was shaky. "I think it followed me home from that awful house."

Billie poured a drink and slid it across the table to her friend. "Did you see it?"

"No. But I can feel it. Watching me." Tammy took a strong gulp. "I felt something touch me. It was awful."

Billie squeezed Tammy's hand to reassure her. Tammy had

always been the skeptic. If she felt something haunting her, then there was a good chance it was real. "We can deal with it."

"How?"

"I'll talk to it. Whatever it is, I'll make it go away."

The scotch in Tammy's glass sloshed around. "What if it doesn't want to go?"

"Leave that to me."

Tammy set the glass down on the table. "I think Kaitlin is in danger."

"Have you heard from her?"

"No." Tammy dug her phone from her back pocket. "Remember the photos I took at the murder house? I was going through them earlier. Here, look at Kaitlin."

Billie took the phone from her and looked at the photograph displayed there. A shot of herself and Kaitlin standing in the ruins of the house but Kaitlin's face was blurred, almost crossed-out by a white smudge. Billie shrugged. "It's just a bad snapshot."

"Look at the rest."

Billie spun through the rest of the shots, some of Kaitlin alone or with Billie. Kaitlin's features were distorted in every photograph. "How many pictures are like this?"

"All of them. And not just the ones from that night. Every photo I have of Kaitlin is like that." Tammy took the phone back. "Did you take any pictures that night?"

She had but in the mayhem of the past two days, Billie hadn't even looked at them. Turning her phone on, she thumbed through the gallery. A handful of snaps from that night. Of the four friends, Kaitlin was the most photogenic, never failing to flash a big, bright smile but here too, in the pictures Billie had taken, Kaitlin's face was distorted and unclear. She turned the screen for Tammy to see.

"What does it mean?"

"It means you're right. She is in danger."

Tammy turned her phone dark, not wanting to see the images anymore. "But why just her? Our faces aren't like that."

"Kaitlin's always had a weird interest in this stuff." Billie hesitated, unsure if her friend really wanted to know but there was no point in being coy about it now. "Something must have latched onto her when we walked into that place. Maybe even before that."

"You make it sound like it's her own fault," Tammy said.

"That's not what I meant," Billie shot back. She didn't like her friend's tone. "She might have been vulnerable to it, that's all."

The air seemed to turn sour. Tammy finished the last of her drink and fell silent.

Billie felt her back get up. "You blame me for this, don't you?"

"I didn't say that," Tammy replied, without looking up.

"You didn't have to."

Tammy took the bottle and splashed more into her glass. "It's all she talks about now. Ever since that day you told us about seeing dead people. She's obsessed with it."

"You can't blame me for that." She watched Tammy pour the tumbler halfway. "Go easy on that."

"Don't tell me what to do."

The sour air lingered. Tammy slugged her drink back. "Maybe we should call Jen."

"Why? She doesn't believe in any of this." That part rankled Billie. Jen rejected any notion of the world that Billie now inhabited. It stung, and that's all there was to it.

From out of the window came the barking of a dog. Incessant and mindless, its racket filled the dead air between them.

Tammy broke the silence first. "What are we going to do?"

Billie said nothing. She got up, took the bottle and returned it to its place atop the fridge. She felt useless and guilty, an awful mix that left her gut feeling queasy.

Her phone went off, buzzing across the kitchen table. She scooped it up. "Hello?"

"She's here." A man's voice, hoarse and brittle.

"Kyle?" Billie snapped her fingers to get Tammy's attention. "What's wrong?"

"She's back," Kyle's voice stammered out. "Kaitlin. But she's not right."

"Is she hurt? Where has she been?"

"There's something wrong with her, Billie. All kinds of wrong."

Tammy jumped out of her chair and leaned into her friend. Billie tilted the phone for her to hear. "Kyle, put Kaitlin on the phone."

"Shhh," he hissed. "She'll hear. She said she's not alone."

"What? Who's with her?"

"I don't know. There's nobody but Kaitlin insists there's a woman with her. One that only she can see." His voice cracked over the line. A sharp sniffle, as if he was crying. "She says others are coming."

"Kyle, listen to me," Billie ordered. "Keep her there. Don't let Kaitlin leave. We're on our way."

A racket of noise poured out of the phone. Kyle's voice gasped and the racket carried on. A pounding noise, as if someone was breaking down the door.

"Shit!" Kyle gulped. "Someone's here."

"Who?"

A crash sounded down the line. A scream and more racket, like a struggle was underway. Billie heard Kyle plead for someone to stop and then his voice cut out. The racket dissipated and silence hissed from the phone.

"Kyle!"

Billie called his name into the phone again but the hiss continued. She felt Tammy's grip tighten on her arm.

A muffled scrape sounded on the other end, followed by the sound of someone breathing into the voice piece.

The hair on Billie's neck bristled. "Kyle?"

No answer. More breathing.

Billie looked up at Tammy, unsure of what to do. She hesitated, then asked, "Who is this?"

"...*hello*..." said a voice. Neither Kyle nor Kaitlin.

"Where's Kyle?" Billie stammered. "What have you done with Kaitlin?"

"...*you must be Billie*..."

"Where is Kaitlin?"

"...*she has been a good little girl*..."

Whatever was hissing into Kyle's phone was not human. That much, Billie could tell. Not anymore anyway. Billie swallowed hard and croaked out one more question. "Who is this?"

"...*me? ...my name is Evelyn*..."

CHAPTER 17

THEIR FOOTFALLS ECHOED through the stairwell as they pounded down to the street. Billie didn't even bother to lock her door behind her but she didn't really need to. Something far more effective than a bolt lock kept her flat safe from intruders. Tammy's car was parked around the corner from Billie's building and they sprinted for it.

"We need to call the police," Tammy said, unlocking the door.

Billie disagreed. "Let's just get there."

Kaitlin's building wasn't far. An old school on Stinson that had been renovated into loft spaces. Tammy floored the pedal, bullying and honking her way through traffic until she skidded into the loading zone before the front door of their friend's building. The front entrance was propped open with a brick, allowing them to barge through and rush the stairs to the second floor.

"Kaitlin!" Tammy hollered as they rushed the apartment. The door was unlocked and they barrelled inside.

Kaitlin's apartment was normally pristine and tastefully decorated. Seeing the wreckage of overturned furniture and broken glass on the floor was a shock. It looked like a windstorm had turned the place upside down.

They found Kyle in the kitchen, splayed and still on the tile floor.

Billie knelt over him and touched his neck. He was alive but not conscious. His lip was bloodied and swelling up fast.

"Is he okay?" Tammy said.

"He's out cold. Find Kaitlin."

Tammy ran out of the room to search the rest of the apartment but they both knew that their friend wasn't here. She returned a moment later and knelt beside Billie.

"She's gone," Tammy panted. "How bad is he?"

"I don't know. He won't wake up." Cradling the young man's head on her knees, she handed Kyle off to Tammy. "Here. You try."

Chasing back into the living room, Billie took a deep breath and opened herself up to what lay on the other side of the thin veil of death. No spirit lingered in the apartment but the dead had been here. And whatever it was, it was not benign. Was it really the ghost of the woman from the Murder House? Evelyn. The fact that it had revealed its name to her was unusual. That this entity had enough power to speak through a phone line was downright frightening. Why would it come after Kaitlin?

Something else snagged her radar. A residual echo of violence but not from the dead. Someone else had been here. There were tiny flashes of pain and the sense of hands pushing her down. Billie was experiencing snippets of whatever happened to Kaitlin. She had been taken.

The signs of struggle were everywhere in the apartment. Among the debris knocked across the floor were tiny droplets of blood. The sight of the blood triggered a memory, flashing hard and sharp before Billie's eyes. Another home overturned, another wreckage left from a struggle. She had been a child then, in her own home and there had been blood on the floor then too. The last time she had seen her mother alive.

"Billie!" Tammy's voice called from the other room.

Kyle was sitting up when Billie returned to the kitchen. He was leaning against Tammy with his face in his hands. Billie couldn't tell if he was crying or just in pain.

"Kyle," she said, kneeling down before him. "What happened?"

No response. Billie gently pulled Kyle's hands from his face. The young man's eyes were bloodshot and glassy, darting around the room like a frightened mouse. His voice was brittle. "Something was here."

"What was it?" Billie took hold of his hands to stop them from shaking. "What did you see?"

He shook his head slowly. "I don't know. It was all dark.

Like a shadow. It felt cold."

Tammy snapped her fingers, trying to get his eyes to focus on her. "Kyle, where is Kaitlin?"

"They took her."

The room went cold. Billie squeezed his hands. "Who took her?"

"I don't know," Kyle hushed. "I heard the door bust in. People rushing inside."

"But you didn't see who it was?"

"No." He winced. His hand raised up, touching the back of his head. "I don't know what happened after that."

Tammy ran her fingers over the back of his skull. "There's a lump here." Her fingertips came away dark with blood.

Billie ripped a dishtowel from the counter and tossed it to Tammy to apply to the man's wound, then she sought out Kyle's eyes again. "Kyle, what did Kaitlin say? Was she hurt?"

"She wasn't herself. At all."

"Why did she come back?"

"She wanted her Ouija board. She said she had a new friend." He rubbed his eyes, trying to concentrate. "A woman. Evelyn."

That name again. It sent a shudder down Billie's spine. She took Kyle by the arm and nodded for Tammy to do the same. "Let's get him on his feet."

"What? Shouldn't he lie down or something?"

"No. Get him walking," Billie said. "Then go next door, get someone to stay with him."

Tammy blanched. "We're not leaving him here."

"We're not staying."

"Are you crazy?" Tammy spat. "We need to call the cops. He needs to go to a hospital."

"The neighbour can do that. We're not waiting for the police."

"What is wrong with you?"

Billie lashed out like a rattlesnake. "The police will keep us here for hours. Do you want that? We need to find Kaitlin. Now."

"How?"

"I know where she is."

CHAPTER 18

THE TENANT NEXT door wasn't happy about being disturbed but he agreed to stay with Kyle until the police arrived. They booked it back to the car.

"So?" Tammy said as she unlocked the door. "Where is she?"

"You might not want to go." Billie dialed a number on her phone. "Hang on."

Billie paced the concrete for a moment before ending the call. She looked at the phone like it was broken. "Why can't I get through?"

"To who?"

"Mockler," Billie replied. She tried the number again. "He'll help us."

"But you said no police."

"He's different. Ugh, it's still not connecting."

"Maybe he turned his phone off," Tammy suggested.

"He's not that far away." Billie opened the passenger door.

"Let's see if he's home."

As the car pulled away from the curb, Billie texted a message to Mockler and kept the phone in hand. She tried to think of what else to do. Was there any way to prepare for what was to come? Bringing a police detective along was the only plan she had. And she wasn't all that sure that he would go along.

Tammy took a sharp turn and accelerated onto Sanford. "Time to spill. Where is Kaitlin?"

"At the Murder House."

Tammy spun a sharp look at her friend. "How do you know that?"

"You sure you wanna know?"

"I wouldn't have asked if I didn't."

Billie watched the houses pass by. "The dead woman I saw at the old house. She had been to Kaitlin's apartment. I could feel her there."

"Oh," Tammy said. "Maybe I didn't want to know."

Billie pointed at something up ahead. "Just up here, where the picket fence is."

Tammy coasted to the curb and Billie looked up at Mockler's house. "His car is in the driveway."

"So what's the plan?" Tammy bent low to see the house on their port side. "He's just gonna come help if you ask nicely?"

"Yup. We go back to the old house. Find Kaitlin. Bring her home." Billie clocked Tammy for her reaction. It wasn't good. A visible shiver at the thought of going back. You and me both, she

136

thought. "Listen, if you don't want to come, I'll understand. You can let me out here and go home. No judgment, no regret."

Tammy chewed her lip, her gaze held out over the dashboard at the quiet street. "I'm in. Whatever happens."

Billie needed to be sure. "I don't know what's going to happen. Or what we'll find."

Tammy threw her door open. "Let's just go. Before I change my mind."

They quick-stepped up the driveway and past the parked vehicle, their heels banging up the wooden steps.

"What if he's not here?" Tammy asked. "What if he's gone down to the pub or something?"

"Then we'll think of something else." Billie banged on the front door.

Tammy gushed, unable to contain the fear bubbling up. "He has a girlfriend, doesn't he? What if she answers the door?"

"Just shut up."

A light switched on inside the house. A shadow loomed before the window in the door and then the door swung back. Billie sank an inch with relief upon seeing Mockler. The look on the detective's face was the inverse; surprise, followed by confusion.

"Billie?" he said. "What are you doing here?"

"I'm sorry to just show up like this," she said sheepishly. "I couldn't get through on the phone."

"It died on me." He nodded a hello to Tammy before turning

back to Billie. "What's wrong?"

"We need your help. Kaitlin's in trouble."

"What kind of trouble?"

"It's kind of a long story. Can I fill you in on the way?"

"Yeah." He waved at them to step inside. "Let me just grab my keys. Come on in."

Billie wavered. She didn't want to go inside but Tammy stepped through and pulled her along. She followed the two of them into the kitchen. The house looked different from the last time she had been here, tidy and well kept but now it seemed in shambles. She noted the boxes stacked against the wall, furniture bound with bubble wrap and duct tape.

Mockler moved through the kitchen in a haphazard fashion, as if he'd just woken up. He shrugged into his jacket and scooped his keys from the bowl on the counter. "How do you know your friend is in trouble?" he asked.

"Her boyfriend called," Tammy offered. "Said Kaitlin had come home but she was acting weird."

"Define weird," he said. "Drunk? Exhausted? Guilty?"

"Troubled," Billie said. "Not herself."

Tammy filled in the rest. "And then someone broke into the apartment and took her."

That snapped his attention up sharp. "She was abducted?"

"The place was trashed. Her boyfriend was unconscious."

"Jesus," he said, patting his pockets for anything missed. "You called the police, right?"

"They're on their way."

"Then you need to go back," he said. "You have to talk to the officers—"

Billie cut him off. "We need to find Kaitlin first. She's in danger."

"Okay. Where do we find her?"

"The Murder House."

He stopped cold. "How do you know?"

"Same reason we didn't wait around for the police," Billie said. "Will you help us?"

"All right." He nodded at something near her. "See that drawer behind you? There should be a flashlight in there. Grab it."

She found the light, tested it. It worked. "Did you bring your gun home?"

"Yeah," he answered, surprised by the question.

"Will you bring it?"

Reaching up into the cupboard, Mockler fetched his service issue and clipped the holster to his belt.

Tammy lingered by the door, feeling a bit like a third wheel. She took in the mess of boxes and emptied shelves in the kitchen. Looking into a half-packed box on the chair, she said: "Are you guys moving?"

Mockler coughed. "Sort of."

Billie startled as if seeing the signs of packing for the first time. "You're moving out? Did you buy a new house?"

"Something like that." He nodded at the door. "Let's go."

Tammy hustled for the porch. Billie held back, wondering why the detective was being so cagey about it. She could understand why they would look for a new home, after what went on in this house. She lowered her voice. "How come you didn't tell me you were moving?"

"I don't know," he said, marching for the front door. "It's kind of complicated."

"What's complicated? You buy a new house, move your stuff." She pushed the screen door open. "You just didn't want to tell me."

"Only one of us is moving out." They came out onto the porch and he clicked his key fob to unlock his vehicle. "We'll take my car. Get in."

This time it was Billie who stopped cold. "What?"

"Come on," Tammy hollered, opening the passenger door and jumping shotgun.

Billie hustled to the car, irked at her friend. "I don't want to sit in the back."

"Tough. Let's go." Tammy climbed in and shut the door.

"Ray?" A voice called after them.

All three of them looked up to see a woman standing on the porch, her arms folded over the thin robe. Christina.

Christina leaned forward, trying to see who was getting into the car. "Where are you going?"

"Give me a second," Mockler said to Billie. He crossed back

to the porch.

Billie dropped into the backseat and closed the door. She watched Mockler stop at the bottom step and speak to Christina. With the car doors closed, she couldn't hear anything.

"Is that his girlfriend?" Tammy asked.

"Yes."

"She's pretty."

She was. Even clad in a man's bathrobe and her hair a mess from getting out of bed. Billie hunkered low in the seat and wondered why it bothered her so. His words kept spinning around in her head. Which one of them was moving out? What had happened?

"She's like model-pretty," Tammy went on.

"Yeah. I get it."

Tammy turned around. "What's eating you?"

"Nothing."

They watched the pair talk for a moment longer and then Mockler returned to the car. The vehicle tilted as he dropped under the wheel and turned the ignition.

Billie chewed her lip. "Is everything okay?"

"Yeah."

Tammy looked at him. "Is your girlfriend wondering where you're going with two girls in the car?"

The car jerked as he backed out of the driveway and then jerked again as he gunned the engine. "Something like that," he said.

CHAPTER 19

"STOP HERE," BILLIE said. "Don't go up the driveway."

Mockler had turned onto the lonely road, the rear wheels fishtailing over the gravel before he accelerated again. The road ahead was dark.

He eased off the pedal and looked over his shoulder at Billie in the backseat. "Why the hell not?"

"Someone's there," she said. "Besides Kaitlin.

The car rolled past the overgrown driveway and pulled to the shoulder. Mockler killed the headlights and all three of them looked up at the dark shape of the old house jutting against the escarpment.

Tammy spun around. "How do you know?"

"Just my gut," Billie answered.

"Who?" Mockler watched the house. "How many?"

"I don't know. But roaring up there might spook them into doing something stupid."

Mockler studied the house, the driveway, the grounds about the old estate. No lights in any of the windows and no vehicles parked out front. Nothing had changed since the last time he had seen it.

Billie threw her door open and climbed out. "What are we waiting for?

"Billie, wait!" He shot a look at Tammy before going after her. "Stay in the car."

She was halfway up the driveway when he stopped her. "Billie, wait. You can't go in there."

Billie pulled her elbow from his grip. "Kaitlin's in there. And she's in trouble."

"I'll handle it. Just let me get some more officers here." His phone had barely begun to recharge before he pulled the plug on it. Enough for one call before it died. It was all he needed.

The crunch of gravel underfoot made them both turn. Tammy ran to catch up. "What are you waiting for?"

"I told you to stay in the car," he snarled at her. He pressed the phone to his ear and stepped away. "Nobody move."

"He's calling in more police," Billie said to Tammy.

Tammy's eyes lifted as she took in the expanse of the big house. Its dark windows seem to stare back at them. "Do you really think she's in here?"

Billie stared at the house also, as if trying to see through the limestone and mortar. "I know she is."

Mockler marched back, dropping his phone into a pocket.

"There's a patrol unit on its way."

"And what?" Billie spat. "We just wait for them?"

"No. I wait for them. You're going back to the car."

Billie threw her hands up and marched toward the house. "For Christ's sakes, Mockler. We can't wait any longer."

"Stop." He snatched her arm again but, this time, refused to let go. "You said yourself someone else is in there. It's not safe. The patrol will be here in a minute. Then I'll go in with them."

"Are you scared?" Billie spun to him. "Is that it?"

"I'm not letting you go in there if it's not safe, Billie. Understand that."

She tugged her arm but he wasn't letting go. "You're hurting me."

"I'll break your arm if I have to."

"Oh my God—" Tammy uttered. "Do you hear that?"

Everyone held their breath. It was a scream. Muffled and distant, ringing off the walls from inside the house. A woman's voice.

"Kaitlin." Billie ran for the entrance. She was yanked back hard.

"Go back to the car! Now!" Mockler pushed Billie into Tammy and sprinted for the side door. Unsnapping the holster on his belt, he drew his sidearm and disappeared inside the house.

Sensing that Billie was ready to bolt after the detective, Tammy hung on. "Don't, Billie."

"We can't just stand here."

"It's his job," Tammy barked, holding tight. "What are we gonna do in there? Get in his way?"

Billie fumed. Tammy's own words kept ringing through her head. This was her fault.

The night air was quiet in the wooded rise of the escarpment. The noise of the city was dampened by the trees around them but a new sound lifted through, faint and far away. Police sirens in the distance.

Her fault, she thought. Kaitlin was in danger from whatever evil was inside this foul building. Mockler was running headlong into danger he could not see. The thought of something bad happening to him was too much to bear.

"Kaitlin needs us. They both do. Come on." She yanked her arm free and marched for the door.

Tammy didn't move. "I can't."

"Yes, you can."

"I can't go back in there," Tammy said. Hot tears spilled down her cheeks. "I'm sorry, Billie."

The sight of the tears startled Billie. She had never seen Tammy cry before. Ever. She was still angry with Tammy but the tears cut the legs out from under Billie's ire.

"When the cops come, show them which way we went in." Billie turned and raced for the door.

~

Crunching over the grit on the floor, her footsteps seemed impossibly loud no matter how soft she tried to tread. The corridor ahead was empty and dark. There was no sign of Mockler. Billie whispered his name but that echoed louder than her footsteps. She was right on his tail, she thought. Where could he be?

Stalking further inside the house, she noticed a dull light glowing up ahead where the hallway intersected with another. Peeking around the next corner revealed the source of the light. Candles on the floor, lit and running the length of the corridor like an airport runway. She listened for a moment but there was no sound. She followed the path of candles to where it ended. The door to the cellar stood open. More candles tapering on the steps, leading the way down.

Of course, it led to the basement, she sighed. It had to. Mockler would have followed the candlelit path down. It took a moment to wind up her courage and plunge down the steps. There were more candles down here, lighting a path through the clutter of broken furniture on the floor. All the way down to the chamber ahead where all the awful things had happened.

Billie clenched her teeth. Since returning to the old house, she had kept herself closed to the dead. She didn't want the distraction. She wasn't here to communicate with the spirits or listen to their tales of tragedy. She was here to find Kaitlin and get out. It wasn't enough. Even with her senses closed, the lost souls trapped inside this terrible place caught wind of her. They drifted in from the shadows or lifted straight out of the floor, circling around her. A man with blackened teeth snarled at her, threatening to kill her while a woman in a maid's uniform pleaded to Billie for help, shrieking that she was trapped in this house and could not leave.

"Go away," Billie hissed. "I can't help you."

The dead gnashed their teeth as Billie clenched up, closing off as much as she could. The phantoms withdrew and when their wails died away, a new sound lifted from the darkness ahead. Voices, low and rumbling from the chamber ahead.

Chanting.

The sound of it triggered some primal fear in her, that droning intonation of voices murmuring from the darkness. She wanted to run.

She whispered Mockler's name again. No reply, no signal that he was here. She wouldn't be so scared if she knew he was down here. What if he was in some other part of the house?

Forcing herself on, she pushed forward along the path until something on the floor caught her eye. Dark and solid in the low light. She retrieved the nearest candle and brought it close.

Mockler's gun lay on the cold stone floor.

CHAPTER 20

BILLIE LIFTED THE gun from the floor and held it gingerly as if it was a fragile thing. She had never fired a gun and kept her fingers away from the trigger piece, worried it might go off in her hand.

"Mockler!" she hissed.

She didn't expect a reply. The chanting in the next room grew louder.

She couldn't do this alone. With Kaitlin already in danger and now Mockler in trouble, there was no way she could save them both. She wasn't cut out for this. Why hadn't the police arrived yet?

Something shuffled in the darkness ahead. She took a step back, lifting a candle to see.

A dark figure doubled over on the floor. The detective.

"Ray," she hissed as she ran to him. "What happened?"

He flinched at her touch, as if jolted. When he looked up, his face was pale and sweaty.

"Easy," she cooed. "It's just me. Are you all right?"

"I don't know what happened." His words were slow and strained. "I got sick."

"It'll pass." She rubbed his back, unsure of what else to do. "Just ride it out."

He swiped his forearm over his mouth. "It just came out of nowhere."

"It's her. The woman who first lived here."

"She's dead," he grumbled.

"I know. She wants something." Billie held the gun out to him. "You dropped this."

"Christ." He took the weapon from her and turned it to one side. The safety was still on. "Brilliant move, huh?"

"Can you stand?"

Mockler got to his feet slowly. His face looked green in the candlelight as he cocked his ear to hear something. "What's that noise?"

"Chanting."

Twenty paces on loomed the doorway to the larger chamber, framed with a glow from the other side. Beyond it, the source of the chanting voices.

Mockler shook the fog from his head and turned to her. "Billie—"

"Don't," she said. "Don't tell me to go back outside. Not

now."

The force in her eyes vouched the fight he'd have on his hands if he insisted. He exhaled loudly. "Stay behind me. And stay quiet."

They edged onward, single file, until they gained the doorway. Mockler leaned forward, then waved her in to take a look. Clutching his arm, she snaked around him.

The chamber was lit with the guttering light from dozens of candles. Hovering in the centre of the room were six figures. Dark and amorphous at first until Billie saw the black robes they wore, their faces hidden under the folds of dark hoods. The figures swayed as they chanted around the pentagram on the floor. Five were positioned over the points of the star but the last stood near the pit at the centre. Like contours conjured out of a nightmare, the hooded figures chanted on, enthralled in some ritual.

It took a moment before Billie clocked the seventh individual among the congregants. Splayed on the floor near the pit was the form of a woman, naked and cold to the world. The hooded figure hovering over her held a long knife or sword that reflected the candlelight in the patina of its broad blade.

Billie jerked back behind the door frame and pulled Mockler after her. "Kaitlin. That's her on the floor."

"Quiet," he said, jamming his fingers against her lips.

She knocked his hand away. "They're going to kill her. Did you see the knife they have?"

Mockler leaned back against the wall and wiped a sleeve over his mouth again. "I counted six of them. I don't know if I can stop them all. Not without someone getting hurt."

The chanting ticked up a notch in its rhythm. The tempo quickening, the urgency building. They peered back into the vast room. The hooded figures were closing in on the unconscious woman at their feet.

"We have to do something," Billie hissed.

He pulled her back and then scanned about the floor, searching for something.

"What are you doing?"

Fetching up something from a pile of debris on the floor, he handed her a length of cast iron pipe. "Here. Use it if you have to."

The metal was heavy in her hands. Could she actually hit someone with this?

"Stay behind me," he said. "If someone comes at you, hit them with that. Ready?"

She nodded, even though it was a lie.

The chanting from the other room stopped.

"Oh shit."

Mockler charged into the chamber with the gun raised in both hands, barking loud and furiously. "Police! On the ground! Now!"

Staying on his tail, Billie knocked into him when the detective stopped suddenly, his bark trailing off.

The hooded figures were gone. All six had vanished into the shadows.

The prone woman remained on the floor inside the pentagram.

"Kaitlin!" Billie ran for her friend but something wasn't right. She dropped to her knees and rolled the woman onto her back.

It wasn't Kaitlin. The same build, same hair as her friend but the woman on the floor was a stranger.

"It's not her," she said. "It's not Kaitlin."

Mockler swept the gun over the room one more time, then knelt down beside Billie. "Is she alive?"

Billie touched the woman's neck, feeling for a pulse. "Yes."

Mockler looked at the woman's face. "Do you know her?"

"I've never seen her before."

The chanting rose up out of nowhere, loud and frighteningly urgent. Billie startled at its ferocity and looked up.

The hooded figures were back, positioned at the points around the pentagram and surrounding them. Carrying on with their ritual. The one with the dagger rushed in, swinging the blade.

Mockler blocked it with his arm and the blade sliced through his jacket, drawing blood. He spun fast and brained the hooded figure in the skull with the butt of the pistol. The others rushed in, swarming them.

Billie shot to her feet, swinging the iron pipe, more than willing to brain every last one of the creepy figures but the one with the dagger slashed at her. The blade sliced across her knuckles and she shrieked in pain and reared back suddenly as the figure slashed at her again.

The gun went off, cracking loud and sharp near her ear. Three times. Pop, pop, pop.

The one with the blade came again but Billie swung the pipe fast and connected hard, bringing the figure down. It splayed across the floor and Billie's blood boiled and she wanted nothing more than to smash the bastard's skull with the pipe. She raised the iron for another swing when the figure rolled over and the hood fell away.

The face of a woman leered up at her, her features twisted up with venom.

"Kaitlin?"

Kaitlin slashed at her again and then something knocked into Billie from behind. All around her was the scrum of Mockler swarmed by the robed congregants. He lashed out in a berserk rage, clubbing and kicking out at the mob. The gun reported in two rapid bursts and then another. Robed figures fell and others scampered into the darkness like cockroaches. Mockler roared like a madman, incomprehensible with rage.

Kaitlin lunged at Billie and the two of them tumbled back and fell into the broken pit in the floor. Billie panicked at being trapped in the hollow that had held the skeleton for so long. She scrambled to get out but she was pinned down under Kaitlin, who had fallen on top of her. A slow hiss leaked out of the crazed woman and the fury in her eyes dimmed rapidly. Billie pushed her off and struggled to clamber out of the narrow space.

Kaitlin collapsed against the wall and her eyes fell to the stomach where the robe was turning red with blood from the dagger stuck in her belly.

"Kaitlin!" Billie thrust her hand over the wound, unsure of whether or not to pull the blade. She left it and tapped Kaitlin's cheek to rouse her. "Kaitlin, look at me. Don't pass out."

The light was fading from the young woman's eyes. Billie had no wish to see Kaitlin's ghost. She screamed at Mockler for help.

The detective lurched across the room with a pronounced limp. One last member of the hooded coven was crawling away on all fours like some wounded animal looking for a place to die. Mockler swung down hard with the pistol and a sharp crack sounded as it connected with the fugitive's skull. The figure fell flat in the folds of its robe.

Mockler swung around and staggered back to Billie, already dialing his phone. His face fell as the phone went dark from the barely charged battery.

"Help her!" Billie roared, grabbing hold of his collar.

He dropped to his knees but, taking in the extent of the wound, he seemed at a loss as to how to help the woman bleeding out onto the flagstones.

Billie fell silent and when her screams ceased echoing off the stone walls, their ears hooked another sound filtering in from outside. The wailing shriek of a police siren.

CHAPTER 21

THE SOUNDS OF of the waiting room grated Billie's nerves. The droning voice over the PA system and the squeak of sensible shoes underscored the throbbing pain in her hand. The cut across her knuckles had been bandaged up but she needed to keep the hand raised to quell the pain throbbing through it.

Billie had never liked hospitals in the first place and that sentiment had only deepened after waking up in one two months ago and learning that she had been in a coma for three days. That was the moment when her whole world had turned on its head. Nothing had been the same since. She watched the doors to the Emergency Room slide open as people shuffled in and stifled the urge to get up and walk out.

"We should just go home," Tammy said, curled up on the chair next to Billie. She let her shoes drop to the floor and tried to get comfortable. "We won't hear anything for hours."

"Yeah," Billie sighed. Neither of them stirred from their

chairs.

They had been told two hours ago that Kaitlin was in critical condition, her injuries severe. They hadn't heard a peep since, despite asking the harried staff for an update.

"We could take shifts," Tammy suggested. "You go home, get some sleep. Come back in a couple hours and relieve me."

"You go. I'll take the first watch."

Tammy didn't move. "Should we try Kyle again?"

"I guess," Billie shrugged. They had called Kaitlin's boyfriend a number of times but he hadn't picked up. For all they knew, he might even be in this very same hospital. Neither of them had a contact number for Kaitlin's parents.

Billie looked up to see Detective Mockler and a uniformed officer appear in the corridor. They spoke quietly for a moment before the uniform nodded and carried on to the exit. The detective scanned the waiting room, clocked the two women and made his way over. His shirtsleeves were rolled up to accommodate the heavy gauze bandaged over the left forearm.

He took a seat across from the two women. "Any word on your friend?"

"Still in critical condition," Billie said. "But that was hours ago."

Mockler noted the bruise on Billie's cheek and the dressing swathed over her knuckles. "How's the hand?"

"Four stitches," Billie replied. She nodded at his own wound. "You?"

He raised his arm. "Stings. I think one of those bastards bit me."

Tammy perked up. "Who were those people anyway?"

"We don't know yet," he said. "Even the two we apprehended. They had nothing on them and they don't speak English."

"What language do they speak?"

"I think it's Norwegian," the detective shrugged. "We're still trying to find a translator."

"They didn't have any ID on them?" Billie asked.

"They weren't even wearing clothes under those robes."

"What about the woman?"

"She's still unconscious. The doc thinks she was drugged."

A call came over the PA system and the three of them sat quietly until it was done. Tammy tucked her feet under her. "What do you think they did to Kaitlin? I mean, why was she with them?"

He looked to Billie before replying, as if she had an answer he didn't. "We don't know. Hopefully, she can fill us in when she wakes up."

"That wasn't her back there," Billie said. "She wasn't herself."

Neither Tammy nor the detective responded, leaving the statement to hang in the air.

Tammy stretched her arms. "Will she be charged with anything?"

"I really can't say at this point." He glanced at Billie. "All depends on how much we can piece together about what happened to her."

Tammy leaned in and lowered her voice. "Billie said there's been other incidents like this. This weirdo devil worship stuff. Is that true?"

Again, he fired a look at Billie but it was a little sharper. "Miss Culpepper shouldn't be talking about stuff like that."

The three of them fell silent for a moment but Mockler seemed unable to sit still, his knee bouncing rapidly.

"You all right?" Billie asked.

"I need to talk to you about something but it can wait," he said. "It's been a long night. Why don't I get someone to drive you two home."

"We're gonna stay. Someone should be here when Kaitlin wakes up." Billie sat up straight and stretched. "We can talk now."

He got to his feet. "Okay. Let's get some air. Excuse us, Tammy."

They passed through the doors into the night where a slight breeze was pushing dry leaves down the sidewalk. They crossed to a bench near the hedgerow and sat down.

"You holding up?"

"I guess," she shrugged. "I feel kind of numb right now."

"That's shock. It'll burn off soon enough. You've had a hell of a night."

"I seem to be having a lot of those." Billie leaned back and looked up at the night sky. There were no stars. "You know, I used to have a normal life. Quiet. Before that night you almost killed me."

"I see. So this is my fault?"

"Yup. You're a bad influence."

He smiled at the joke, but only for a second. He still seemed fidgety.

"Okay," Billie sighed. "What is it?"

He reached into a pocket and placed something on the bench between them. A long stick and cap sealed in clear plastic.

She picked it up, the packaging crinkling in her hand. "What is it?"

"It's a swab stick. For DNA sampling."

Now she was confused. "You want my DNA?"

He nodded. "It's about the remains you found in the basement. Remember I said we found some moldy ID with it? The lab was able to recover some of the print."

She sat up, even more confused. "And? Who is he? Or she?"

The detective scratched his chin, something she'd seen him do a hundred times before. Stalling before delivering bad news.

"According to the ID, his name was Franklin Riddel."

The name snagged in her ear, like an alarm tripping. Something from a long, long time ago. "Riddel?"

"I ran the name through the system," Mockler said. "It came back with a big red flag. Franklin Riddel was married, briefly, to one Mary Agnes Culpepper."

A sharp click sounded in Billie's ear. She couldn't breathe. "That's my mother's name..."

"Billie, he's your father." He settled his hand over her wrist. "He's also the man wanted for the disappearance of your mother twenty years ago."

The numbness crept back as the rug was suddenly yanked from under her feet.

Franklin Riddel was a name without a face. A father she never knew, rarely mentioned by a mother whom Billie had lost when she was a child. None of this made sense and she wished the man next to her would stop talking. What was he saying?

"I don't know what to make of it either," Mockler said. "Somehow you located his remains. But how did he end up there?"

"It has to be a mistake," she said.

"That's why I brought the swab kit. To be sure."

Dead leaves tumbled around their ankles and blew off down the concrete. Neither spoke for a long time.

Mockler turned when he heard a sob. He moved the kit out of the way and put his arm around her. "I thought this all started in June when I knocked you into the harbour. But it goes back much farther than that."

"Yes." She let her head rest against his shoulder.

He let out a long breath. "Okay. Why don't we get some coffee and then go back to the beginning. And start there."

"Can we just sit here for a bit?" she said.

"Sure."

A leaf fluttered down from above and settled onto her knee, dry and brittle as paper. Billie reached for it but the wind swept it up again before she could catch it.

AFTERWORD

Do you believe in ghosts?

A simple question. A timeless question. Around how many campfires has it been asked, the questioner and questioned staring at one another across the flames?

My answer? Maybe. Sometimes.

I never used to. Despite a lifelong passion for horror and the supernatural, I never for a moment believed that any of it was real. Or even possible. It was all just good spooky fun. Sort of like church.

Growing up, I had aunts on my dad's side who believed in all kinds of things. They relished anything spooky and supernatural but most of all, they loved 'true tales' of the unexplained. Ghost stories and hauntings and tales of poetic comeuppance. This, I should add, was also the deeply Catholic side of the family so there may be some correlation there. I dismissed them as eccentric. Possibly mad too.

These days, I'm not so certain about the whole paranormal

thing. My skepticism has worn away incrementally over the years. Now, as a husband, father and pulp writer, I find that I want to believe more and more. Is it just age, creeping up like arthritis in the bones? Or is it the same impulse that drives the elderly back to the church; the fear of death. Or the judgment that might come after that.

Ah see, there's that old-time Catholicism creeping back in when I'm not looking. Like a mouse facing the coming winter, it will sneak its way into the house through any crevice it can find.

There wasn't any single event that changed my mind. It was a sliding scale of small events that stacked up over time. To be fair, these things may all have been coincidence that my feeble mind decided to string together as cause and effect.

Five years ago we renovated the basement of our house and I think I may have disturbed something in the process. Tearing out a section of the broken concrete floor, I unearthed a small bone from the musty dirt. Measuring about seven inches long, it appeared to be a leg bone to my untrained, non-expert eye. The bone could have belonged to a medium sized animal, like a goat or a dog. Maybe even a pig. It could also, I believed, be human.

What was it doing under the slab cellar floor of a Victorian rowhouse built in 1896? I had no idea but apparently, this wasn't the first incident of skeletal remains found here. Other small bones had been uncovered years before when the old boiler had been removed to make way for a modern forced-air furnace.

According to local lore, it wasn't uncommon for early 20th century homeowners to bury animal bones under the dirt of their bare-earth cellars. I have no idea why they would do such a thing, nor have I been able to confirm this tidbit of local lore.

It's possible that this lonely bone is all that remains of some poor lamb butchered for some holiday feast by the original home-owners of the late 1800's. I simply don't know. After digging it up, I washed the thing and showed it to my daughters, joking that I had unearthed the ghost of old Mrs. O' Malley. (Don't ask me who old Mrs. O' Malley is, it just sounded right at the time. I do remember reading that children's classic *The Teeny-Tiny Woman* around that time). Neither daughter thought it was very funny at the time. The missus even less so.

The incidents after that were small but odd. Our youngest would sometimes talk to an imaginary friend. Other times, she refused to go to another floor by herself, scared of something she couldn't articulate.

The cat, who rules the house, balked at a certain section of the basement, refusing to go anywhere near the spot where the bone was uncovered.

Neither of these two incidents are significant. Cats are just strange and childhood fears are common. The clincher for me was the voice in my ear. A sunny summer afternoon and a quiet house. My wife was out with the kids and I was alone. Sitting on the front stoop after mowing the lawn, something hissed into my ear and I damn near jumped out of my skin. There was no one there (not even the obnoxious cat). But the voice was unmistakeable and as loud as bombs as if someone had hissed right into my ear. To this day I'm not even sure what the voice said. Something simple and non-threatening. My name or 'hey' or 'you'. But it scared the hell out of me and that awful voice put a chill down my spine like nothing else before.

Unable to shake the creepy feeling, I began drawing connections to the events. The bone and my daughter's fears. Her imaginary friend and the odd behaviour of the cat in the renovated basement. The awful voice in my ear and old Mrs. O' Malley.

With a new slab floor poured and a fake hardwood floor installed over that, I had no way of returning the little bone to its original place of internment. Flustered, I buried it in the front garden, down amongst the roots of the aging rose bushes.

After that, the weird incidents stopped. Or my feeble mind stopped drawing conclusions around unrelated events. Yet the erosion of skepticism continued and the possibility of the paranormal became more real and it all led here, to *The Spookshow*.

Where do stories come from? In my experience, it's often a mish-mash of stuff stewing in the back of the brain until the pot boils over. One of those elements was a fondness for paranormal reality TV shows. *Psychic Kids* was a favourite, where adult mediums would mentor kids with psychic abilities learn to understand their own unique talents. Most of the kids featured on that program could see or sense the dead around them and what was fascinating (and heartbreaking at the same time) was how terrifying that would be to a child. Unable to understand what they were experiencing, these children often withdrew into themselves. Their schooling would suffer and they would lose friends and become isolated as the world around them became frightening. The parents of these poor kids were at their wit's end, unable to understand or help their child. Most episodes ended on a happy note as the adult psychic would give the child tools to cope with the spirit world. I knew from the first episode that I saw that a child with sensitivities would make for a great story but the idea never went anywhere. It stayed in the brain and stewed.

An even bigger influence is *The Dead Files*. If you're familiar with that show, you might recognize the influence in the pairing of a psychic and a cop in the *Spookshow*. I find Amy Allen (the psychic on the *Dead Files*) really compelling in how she physically reacts to the paranormal entities she encounters. She may not be the most articulate person, and she curses a fair deal, but it's all part of the charm for me. The cop on the show, a retired homicide detective, uncovers very strange and startling history behind the places the pair investigate. Ghosts, crimes, and mysteries...what's not to love?

So, back to the timeless question. Do you believe in ghosts?

I want to know. Do you think it's hokum or is there some truth to it? Have you ever had a paranormal or unexplainable experience? Let me know. You can email me at mcgregor (dot) tim (at) gmail.com.

I love a good ghost story.

Toronto

February 2015

Tim McGregor is an author and screenwriter. He lives in Toronto with his wife and children. Some days he believes in ghosts, other days not so much. Find out more at:

timmcgregorauthor.com

or

facebook.com/TimMcGregor

CPSIA information can be obtained
at www.ICGtesting.com
Printed in the USA
LVHW081921300819
629535LV00016B/470/P